Roxbury Park Dog Club

WHEN THE GOING GETS RUFF

DAPHNE MAPLE

HARPER
An Imprint of HarperCollins*Publishers*

To Laura

Roxbury Park Dog Club #2: When the Going Gets Ruff

For information address HarperCollins Children's Books, a division of HarperCollins Publishers, 195 Broadway, New York, NY 10007.
www.harpercollinschildrens.com

Library of Congress Control Number: 2015958595
ISBN 978-0-06-232769-7 (pbk.)

Typography by Jenna Stempel
16 17 18 19 20 OPM 10 9 8 7 6 5 4 3 2 1

First Edition

1

"I just heard about the greatest pet," I said to my mom. We were sitting in the breakfast nook of our sunny kitchen eating English muffins; it was the perfect time to reveal my latest plan to convince my mom we needed a pet.

Mom was taking a long sip of coffee but she looked at me over the rim of her mug and raised her eyebrows, waiting for me to go on.

I took a deep breath. "A de-scented skunk," I announced.

My mom made a sputtering noise as she tried to

keep from choking on her coffee.

I hid my grin by taking a bite of English muffin. This was exactly the reaction I was hoping for.

"A skunk?" Mom asked, her voice shrill. "People actually welcome skunks into their homes?" She glanced around at our immaculate kitchen, where everything was in its place and every surface was free of dust and crumbs. My mom was all about our house being clean, which was why she had shot down every request I'd ever made for a pet.

But I was determined that this time would be different.

"Yeah," I said. "They're very affectionate."

My mom shuddered at the thought of cuddling with a skunk.

"And they're clean," I adding, laying it on thick.

She shook her head. "There is no way we are getting a skunk."

"Okay," I mumbled in my most disappointed voice, slumping down in my seat but casting a quick glance at my mom. Just as I'd hoped she looked concerned. Yeah, my mom had a ton of rules about cleaning and homework and screen time, but I knew how much she wanted me to be happy. Ever since she and my dad had split up when I was a baby it was just the two of us and I knew how hard she worked to get me things like American Girl dolls, and send me to summer camp and dance classes. But the thing I wanted more than anything was a pet, which was why I'd come up with this whole plan in the first place. It was never about a skunk, it was about a—

"Well, then what about a hamster?" I asked, like the thought had just occurred to me. "Hamsters live in a cage and look cute."

"Their cages need wood shavings," my mother said, frowning slightly at the thought of the dust wood shavings might create.

"Actually now they have paper shavings that hardly make a mess at all," I replied. I'd done my research.

"What about the odor?" my mom asked, wrinkling

her nose as though she could already smell a dirty hamster cage.

"We could keep the cage in my room," I said. "And I'd clean it every day so it would stay fresh."

My mom stood up and began to clear her place. "Hurry up with that English muffin, honey," she said. "You don't want to be late."

I was so eager to do what she asked that I stuffed the rest of my food in my mouth. Then I saw her wince. Whoops. Yes, I'd finished the muffin, but I'd forgotten to use good table manners, one of the many things that mattered to my mom. Honestly sometimes it was hard to get everything just how my mom wanted it. It didn't help that she was perfect, from her neat clothes and our spotless house to her job as a successful lawyer. I got my less-than-perfect genes from my dad, who lived in Seattle. When I visited him during school vacations there were dishes piled in the sink, comfortable clutter on every surface, and we always chewed with our mouths open. Not that I'd want to live with my dad; I was happy here in Roxbury Park. But it might be nice if just once in a while my mom relaxed enough to leave a few crumbs on the counter or something.

"Really, Mom, you wouldn't even know the hamster was there," I said as I rinsed off my dishes in the sink and piled them neatly in the dishwasher, trying to make up for the muffin thing.

"A pet is a lot of work," my mom said, filling a travel mug with coffee for her drive to work. She added a half teaspoon of sugar and then secured the lid.

"I know, but I would do it all," I said. "I'd use my allowance to buy hamster food, I'd change the water every day, I'd clean the cage, everything."

My mom glanced at the clock on the stove. "We'd better hurry or we'll be late," she said.

For a moment I wondered if I should let it go and wait until later to push for the hamster. I didn't want to make us late. But I'd come this far and the skunk decoy really seemed to have worked. I needed to see it through now, before my mom could come up with other reasons not to get the hamster.

"Okay," I said, following my mom down the hall to the foyer. I'd left my pink backpack in its designated spot on the bench by the door, next to the rack where we kept all our shoes. Inside the house we did socks and slippers only. "But Mom, what about the hamster? I really think I'm ready for a pet. I'm old enough to take care of it all on my own and I promise you won't have to do a thing."

I held my breath as I waited for her to answer. Last week when my mom was in line to pay for our groceries I'd gone to the pet store next door. At the big hamster cage I'd picked out the one I wanted, a girl with feather-soft tan and white fur. I was going to name her Pippi, after my favorite book character. And now as I waited I imagined how great it would be, coming home to Pippi every day, watching her run on her wheel and snuggle down in her paper shavings every night.

My mom was putting on a pair of black high heels. "Honey, no," she said, the one word puncturing all my hopes.

"But why?" I knew I was whining, which my mom hated, but I couldn't help it. I could practically feel Pippi's cuddly little body in my hands and I wasn't ready to let that go without a fight.

My mom pulled on the blue blazer that went with the suit she was wearing, then looked at me and sighed. "Sash, I know how much you want a pet," she said. "But I don't think you're ready. A pet is a huge responsibility: it's a living creature and it depends on you completely."

"I can handle it, I know I can," I said quickly. I was positive I could, if only she would give me a chance.

But my mom was shaking her head. "Last week you forgot to take out the trash and it made the whole kitchen smell," she said.

"Right, but that was just a one-time thing because I had that big math test to study for," I explained.

"And two weeks ago you forgot your essay for English class and I had to leave work to bring it in so you wouldn't fail the assignment," she went on.

I opened my mouth to remind her that the real problem there was my insanely strict English teacher, Mrs. Benson, who never allowed late work. And I had gotten an A on the essay so you could argue that it had all worked out in the end.

But clearly my mom wasn't looking at it that way. "Then yesterday you forgot to take the lasagna out of the freezer and we had to go out to dinner because it wasn't thawed in time."

I was about to say that we would never have problems like that if she'd just break down and get a microwave, something she refused to do because she said it changed the way food tasted. But my mom held up a hand. "And then there was this weekend when you forgot to tell me that you promised Dana we'd give her a ride to dance and she ended up missing the class."

Okay, that one was pretty bad.

"Mom, everyone forgets things sometimes," I said, trying to sound mature.

My mother was nodding. "That they do, my love," she said. "But some people forget things a lot. A whole lot. And those people aren't ready for a pet. I'm sorry, but that's just how it is."

This time my shoulders slumped for real. I couldn't believe that me forgetting a few things—okay, maybe more than a few—meant no Pippi. But it was clear that my mom thought I was too scatterbrained to handle a pet. And it was equally clear that she considered the topic closed.

"Now get a move on," my mom said briskly. "Or you'll be late."

Unfortunately that was when I remembered that I'd forgotten my sweater upstairs. I raced up to get it, then stuffed my feet into my pink sneakers and flew out the front door. If I ran I still had time to catch my best friends, Kim and Taylor. The three of us met on the corner of Spruce and Montgomery every morning so that we could walk to school together.

But just as I jumped down the front steps, ready to

sprint down the wide stone path to the sidewalk, my mom called me.

I turned and she silently held up my backpack, which I'd left on the bench, pretty much proving her point that I was kind of absentminded.

Whoops.

"Thanks, Mom," I said, running back up the steps to get the backpack.

There was no way I was going to win the pet debate today. But as I raced down the sidewalk I was already planning my next argument, and this one wouldn't fail.

Because I wasn't going to give up until I had a pet of my own.

2

I was panting when I reached the corner but Kim and Taylor were still there, heads bent together as they chatted. I loved seeing them so happy together. Not long ago, when Taylor moved here at the start of the school year, they weren't quite as friendly. In fact they were downright unfriendly. Kim had been my best friend since kindergarten but then I met Taylor last summer when my mom and I were up at Lake George, and we totally hit it off. I was thrilled when she told me that her family was moving to Roxbury Park so her dad could work at my mom's law firm. But Kim was pretty much the opposite of thrilled and Taylor wasn't exactly excited about Kim either. After a few days I was starting to think they'd never hit it off. But then a group of dogs saved the day and we've been the three musketeers ever since.

"Hey, Sasha," Kim said, turning and smiling at me, her brown eyes warm.

"How'd the skunk plan go?" Taylor asked, pushing one of her braids out of her eyes. Taylor had brown skin and her hair was done up in a hundred little braids decorated with gold beads that made a musical clinking when she moved her head.

"Yeah, are you going to get Pippi?" Kim asked as we started off toward Roxbury Park Middle School.

"No," I said with a sigh.

Kim squeezed my arm sympathetically.

"The skunk decoy seemed so perfect," Taylor said regretfully.

My friends knew how much I wanted a pet and they'd helped me concoct my latest plan. Loving animals, especially dogs, was one of the many things we had in common. Actually a dog was the pet I wanted most of all, but my mom had said a firm no to that long ago, so now I was just trying to get her to agree to anything! And so far I was having no luck.

"Yeah, I thought so too," I said. "But my mom didn't go for it."

"She does love a clean house," Kim said.

In the past that was why my mom had always vetoed a pet. Today was the first time she'd ever said that my forgetfulness was part of the problem too. I opened my mouth to tell my friends but then closed it. Knowing my mom thought I was irresponsible made me feel humiliated and pathetic, like a little kid who can't handle tying her own shoes or making her own bed. And I didn't feel ready to talk about that yet.

"Don't give up," Taylor said. "You'll figure out a pet she'll agree to."

"And then you can name it Pippi," Kim said comfortingly.

Even if they didn't know the whole story they always made me feel better.

"And we have the shelter today," Taylor added, cheering me up even more.

One of the cool things about seventh grade was that everyone had to do some kind of after-school volunteer work and the three of us worked at pretty much the most awesome place around: the Roxbury Park Dog Shelter. It was my favorite part of the week, getting to hang out with dogs and my best friends.

"You have your shelter clothes, right?" Kim asked with a grin.

I rolled my eyes. My mom hated the thought of dog fur in our house so part of getting her to agree to let me work at the shelter (which took most of last summer) was my promise that I'd change clothes when I was there. My mom always washed my shelter clothes as soon as I got home and so far no dog fur had touched a single thing in our house. "Yes, but I almost forgot my backpack," I said.

My friends laughed and I tried to join in, only it was a little harder than usual. Now that I knew my mom thought my forgetfulness meant I wasn't ready to have a pet, it wasn't quite as funny as it had been before.

"So are you guys ready for the new dog today?" Kim asked as we waited for the light to change on Main Street. The leaves were just starting to turn so the trees were lit up gold and crimson in the morning sun.

"Sierra? She had a lot of energy when she came on Saturday," Taylor said a bit uncertainly. Taylor'd had a secret when she signed up to work at the shelter: she was afraid of big dogs. I had no idea but Kim not only figured it out, she helped Taylor so that now she's comfortable with all the dogs. And that's how Taylor and Kim became friends.

"Don't worry," Kim told Taylor. "She'll settle down. She'll fit into the club in no time."

The three of us had started the Roxbury Park Dog

Club a few weeks ago. It was for dogs who needed a little extra playtime because their owners worked long hours. For a fee the dogs would come play at the shelter for the afternoon, kind of like a doggy after-school program. So far it was a big success and super fun. And it was always exciting when a new dog signed up. Taylor was definitely right about Sierra though—she was pretty rambunctious. When she'd come in for her first meeting with the shelter dogs she'd raced around wildly, starting a dog mob with half the shelter dogs streaking after her and the others cowering in the corners. But she was only two and still had some puppy habits, such as getting overstimulated in new settings. Like Kim I was sure she'd calm down once she got used to the routine.

"Did Sierra's family sign up for pickup service?" Taylor asked me. We all had roles in the club and I was in charge of taking new client calls, and managing our client list and the scheduling.

"No, her owners thought it was best to drop her off themselves," I said. We offered a pickup service where we'd get the dogs from home and bring them to the club, but the Finnegans were going to bring Sierra over themselves, at least for now.

"Probably a good idea," Taylor said with a shudder, no doubt remembering that dog mob.

"She'll do great once she settles in," I said, patting Taylor's arm. "And remember, if we have any problems, we can just pull out our secret weapon."

Taylor nodded, grinning, but Kim's eyebrows scrunched together.

"What's our secret weapon?" she asked.

"You," I said, smiling. "Our resident dog whisperer."

"You guys are great with the dogs too," Kim said quickly, her cheeks turning pink. She always had trouble taking compliments.

"We are," I said cheerfully. "But you're the master." She really was. Honestly sometimes it seemed like Kim spoke the secret language of dogs, always able to know just what they needed the second they needed it.

"Agreed," Taylor said. Every once in a while her Southern accent shone through, reminding us where she was from. "Do y'all think we'll have a quiz in English today?"

Mrs. Benson was very fond of pop quizzes.

"I hope not," I said. "I kind of skimmed the last few chapters." We'd just started reading *The Good Earth* and so far I liked it, but last night I'd been too busy researching hamsters to read it carefully enough for one of Mrs. Benson's quizzes.

"I hope not either," Kim said, biting her lip. Sometimes she struggled a little in school. Her parents made sure she spent her three free afternoons a week on homework, which Kim hated, of course, but it did help her get most assignments done on time. And she got to do her homework in her family's awesome diner, the Rox, which had the best sweet potato fries in the world. Not to mention the best apple pie. Sometimes her older brother, Matt, helped her out too. I was a little jealous of both Taylor and Kim because they had siblings and I was an only child. But Taylor said being the youngest of four girls was the worst and Kim said her older brother constantly smelled like old socks, so maybe I was the lucky one.

"She just gave us one yesterday," I said as we started up the path to school. Kids were scattered over the lawn, talking in groups and moving slowly toward the big metal doors. "Hopefully she won't give us two in a row."

Taylor raised her eyebrows. "This is Mrs. Benson we're talking about," she said. Then she raised her voice in a near-perfect imitation of our teacher. "You will meet the standards required of a seventh grade student and present work befitting that standard or else it's off with your head!"

I laughed and Kim gave a half smile, but she still looked worried.

"I bet you'll have time to look it over in homeroom," I told her, deciding I'd do the same. No normal teacher would give two pop quizzes in a row, but like

Taylor said, Mrs. Benson was no normal teacher.

The five-minute bell rang as we walked up the steps and into the school.

"Hey, guys," our friend Rachel called as she passed, ducking around three boys playing keep-away with a fourth boy's baseball cap.

We waved at her and then at a group of girls in our social studies class who were headed in the other direction. Mornings at Roxbury Park Middle School were always a mob scene, but at least it was a friendly mob scene.

"See you guys in homeroom," Taylor said, turning into the alcove where her locker was.

"See you there," Kim and I called, and then a moment later Kim stopped at her locker.

I threaded my way through the mass of people, down the hall that was papered with posters announcing different club meetings and sporting events to attend. I kind of wished I had time to join girls' volleyball—the team was really good—or sign up for the musical. But

I was busy enough with dance classes and the shelter. And of course researching different pets to find the one my mom would finally allow.

Because that was my most important activity of all.

3

"Who's a sweet boy?" I crooned to Gus, a playful chocolate Lab who was jumping around as I let myself into his house. As soon as I was in he ran over to be petted, his whole body wriggling in delight.

I sat on the floor so I could give him a good rub and he butted his head gently against me, panting happily.

There was nothing in the world as wonderful as doggy love!

After a few minutes I got up and grabbed his leash, which was on the hall table, right where his owners always left it for the walk to Dog Club. I snapped it on Gus's collar and off we went. I almost forgot to lock the front door but I remembered before we were even off the porch, so it didn't really count.

"Are you looking forward to seeing your friends?" I asked Gus, who bounced along happily next to me. I knew the answer to the question—all the club dogs loved their time at the shelter. Instead of being stuck home alone they had dogs to run with and people to play with. It was the perfect solution for dogs who got lonely.

But it had also been the perfect solution for the shelter. When we first started working there we learned that Alice, the owner, was running out of money. If she didn't find a new source of income, the shelter would have to close. It was Kim who came up with the brilliant plan of the Dog Club. At first Alice wasn't sure, but we convinced her, with help from the two other shelter volunteers, Tim and Caley. And now lonely dogs had a place to play and the Roxbury Park Dog Shelter had a way to stay in business.

"Look, your friends are here," I told Gus, who was already heading toward the dog park. When we first started the club we'd arrived at the shelter with all the club dogs together and it was total mayhem. Now we each went to pick up our assigned dogs and then met up at the dog run. We'd let the dogs play for a few minutes so that when we arrived at the shelter they were a lot calmer. The whole thing was Kim's idea of course, and like all her ideas involving dogs, it was terrific.

"Hey," Taylor called as Gus and I walked up. She was already there with Humphrey and Popsicle. Humphrey, a sleepy bassett hound, was the very first club dog, and Popsicle had actually been a shelter dog until Humphrey's owners had adopted her. She was a sweet little black and white puppy, though as we came up I realized she wasn't quite as small anymore.

"Popsicle's getting big," I said as I let Gus greet his friends.

"And more energetic," Taylor said, rubbing her arm. "She pulled me all the way here."

The three dogs were sniffing happily when Kim arrived with Coco, a big brown and black dog with floppy ears and a tendency to run whenever she could. It took a firm hand to manage Coco, which was why Kim picked her up.

"Someone's ready to play," Kim said as they came over, Coco jumping up happily at the sight of her friends. "Down," Kim said firmly, and like magic, Coco settled down and began sniffing instead of leaping.

"Amazing," Taylor said.

We let the dogs play for a few more minutes, then headed to the shelter.

"I wonder if Sierra is here yet," Kim said as we opened the door to the shelter. But the dogs that raced to greet us were our usual shelter dogs, along with Daisy, a brown dachshund whose owner dropped her off for the club. Lily, a mix with shaggy tan fur, came first, followed by Boxer, who was, of course, a boxer. Right behind them was Hattie, a large fuzzy puppy who used to be shy but had gotten a lot braver lately. Kim had been helping with that. Oscar gave a mew from his perch on the windowsill. Oscar was actually a cat, with bright green eyes and silky gray fur, but he thought he was a dog and no one told him otherwise. All three dogs ran straight to Kim, but one dog, a little white Cavachon who was nearly blind, came right to me.

"Mr. Smashmouth," I said joyfully, reaching down to scoop him up. He greeted me with a kiss on my cheek, then snuggled in under my chin, a delicious fluffy bundle in my arms.

"He sure loves you," Taylor said, grinning at me.

"It's mutual," I said. I adored all the shelter and club dogs, but Mr. Smashmouth was special.

"Hi, girls," Alice said, coming out of her little office. Her hair was in its usual messy ponytail and as always she had on a dog shirt. This one said "It's a Dog

Eat Dog World" and had a cartoon of a dog munching on a hot dog.

As we greeted Alice we let the club dogs off their leashes. Popsicle bounded over to Hattie and Daisy while Gus and Coco began a spirited game of chase with Boxer. Humphrey lay down on the floor, in typical lazy bassett fashion, as though the walk here had exhausted him. I knew he'd be up and playing soon.

"Sasha, I think you forgot something," Kim said gently.

I looked at her blankly.

"Your shelter clothes," she said.

Yikes! Mr. Smashmouth had rushed up to me so fast I hadn't had time to change. Lucky for me Cavachons don't shed much, but I'd have to pick off any stray fur before I went home. I grabbed my backpack and headed for the bathroom next to the food storage area. The dogs always looked up hopefully when any of us went in that direction, but then continued playing if we just went into the bathroom instead of to the food.

Aside from the food storage, bathroom, and Alice's office, which was tucked in the back, the shelter was one big room, with cages on one side, where the dogs slept, and a wide-open space for playing. Next to the cages were shelves where the toys were kept, though by this time of day half the toys were strewn about the room or out in the big backyard. Back when we'd first started at the shelter most of the toys were pretty chewed up. But thanks to the Dog Club there were brand-new balls, braided ropes for tugging, and lots of chew toys.

I changed into my faded jeans and my favorite T-shirt ever—the one that said Roxbury Park Dog Club. Alice had made them for us when we first started the club and we all tried to wear them to the shelter. I folded my school clothes, tucked them into my backpack, and then went back out, almost tripping over Mr. Smashmouth, who was waiting for me.

"You are the sweetest," I told him, bending down to scoop him up again. He snuggled in my arms with a contented sigh as I walked to put my backpack in Alice's office, as far away from dog fur as possible.

When I came back out Kim and Taylor were throwing tennis balls and all the dogs except Mr. Smashmouth were chasing after them. The front door opened and in walked Caley and Tim.

"Hey," Tim said, his shaggy black hair falling in his face as he bent down to greet Boxer and Lily, who broke away from fetch to greet him.

"Afternoon, all," Caley said, smiling at us. "I'm glad it's a club day. Things are slow when you guys aren't around."

Caley, with her red curls, cool thrift-shop clothes, and confident manner, was exactly how I hoped I'd be in high school. Well, with my own boring brown hair and new clothes because my mom would never let me wear used clothes. But I loved how self-possessed and friendly Caley was. Plus you could just tell she never forgot things like lasagnas that had to be taken out of the freezer. At first I'd been kind of intimidated hanging out with her and Tim, since they were high school students and all. But they'd been so supportive of the Dog Club idea, and so helpful, that now it just felt normal.

"I wish every day was Dog Club day," Kim said with a sigh. I could tell she was thinking of those three afternoons a week when she was doing homework instead of playing here with the dogs.

"Dog Club days are the best," Tim agreed as Coco raced over and nearly knocked him down. "Way more exciting than regular days," he added with a laugh.

"If you want excitement I think we're going to get it," Alice said in her gentle way. "Sierra will be a handful."

I felt a tiny twinge of worry at her words. Alice was amazing with all the dogs—in fact she was a lot like Kim. So to hear her say Sierra would be a challenge felt different than when Taylor said it. But I shook it off. Yes, Sierra was energetic. But we were more than ready to handle it.

"We're on it," Caley said as she tossed the now-soggy tennis ball for Boxer and Lily. "And Sierra's going to have a great time."

"How about we start off with some time out back,"

Kim said, already planning how to best handle things. "That way if she's a little wild she can run it off outside, maybe with Boxer and Lily."

"Sounds like a plan," Tim agreed.

"Taylor, you should get your camera ready," Kim went on. "So we can have some pictures of Sierra's arrival for the blog." While my club job was the client list and scheduling, Kim and Taylor did the Dog Club Diary, a blog about what happened in Dog Club so that owners would know what their dogs were up to. Kim wrote short posts and Taylor was the webmaster, as well as the official photographer.

"Right," Taylor said, heading over to her backpack to get her camera. She was pretty into photography and always had it with her.

"Do you think we should take a few of the dogs out now, so not all of them are here when Sierra arrives?" Caley asked Kim.

I loved that even the high school students wanted Kim's advice on dogs.

Kim was nodding. "Yeah, let's do that."

"I think it might be too late," Alice said, cocking her head to one side as though she heard something.

And a moment later I heard it too: the sound of a dog's nails scratching wildly as she raced up the front steps. Which could only mean—

"Sierra's here!" I said, eager to welcome our newest club member.

Taylor grabbed her camera and I headed for the door, ready to greet Sierra. But the moment I opened it, Sierra leaped up, her paws nearly hitting Mr. Smashmouth, still cuddled under my chin. He let out a surprised bark and Sierra tore past me, running wildly around the shelter. She was a big German shepherd mix, so the other dogs, even Boxer and Coco, jumped out of the way as she tore past, ears flying and paws thumping around the room.

"Sierra," Mr. Finnegan called, hurrying in after his dog. His neat gray suit had several muddy dog prints on it and there was a leaf stuck in his hair. Clearly the walk here hadn't gone well.

"Sierra, sit," Kim called in her most serious voice.

We all waited, knowing what would happen: Sierra would slow, Kim would repeat the command, and then Sierra would obey. That was what always happened when Kim used her most serious voice.

But this time it didn't. This time Sierra just kept racing around the room, sending Hattie skittering for the safety of her cage. Gus, Popsicle, and Humphrey cowered in a corner, while Boxer and Coco revved up in hot pursuit.

Uh-oh.

Taylor, Kim, and I exchanged a panicked glance.

"I'm sorry," Mr. Finnegan said, rubbing his forehead. "We're not quite sure why she's still so wild. We expected it when she was a puppy but she's nearly two."

Sierra skidded along the linoleum floor and crashed into the toy shelves. All of us gasped but she barely missed a beat, just took off across the room again.

"Should we see if she's hurt?" Caley asked.

Sierra streaked past.

"I think she's fine," Alice said. "But perhaps we should do as Kim suggested and take her outside."

"Good idea," Mr. Finnegan said. "Though don't expect that to tire her. She can run for hours and still be going strong."

Kim was biting her lip and even Alice was frowning a bit. That definitely didn't sound good.

"All right, dog pack, let's go," Tim, who was closest to the back door, said heartily. The second he opened the door, Sierra thundered toward it. Taylor was half hiding behind Kim as the huge dog flew past, followed by Coco and Boxer, who was more amped up than I'd ever seen him. Lily followed more slowly but none of the other dogs budged. Clearly if Sierra was going outside, they were staying in.

I glanced toward the windowsill and wasn't surprised to see that Oscar's red cat bed was empty. Chances were he was hiding under the sofa in Alice's office, his go-to space when the dogs got too wild. I was guessing we wouldn't see even the tip of his gray tail until Sierra was headed back home.

"Who's coming with me?" Tim asked. His voice was steady but he was cracking his knuckles, something I'd never seen him do before.

Sierra really had all of us on edge.

"I'll go," I announced. The sooner I got comfortable with Sierra the better. I knew she had to be a sweetie under all that exuberance—pretty much all dogs were.

"Me too," Kim said.

We both glanced at Taylor. Sometimes we did our own thing at the shelter but in general when one of us went outside to run around with the dogs, the other two followed.

Taylor was looking like she had just seen a werewolf, not a slightly out-of-control German shepherd. I knew her answer before she even opened her mouth. "I think I'll stay behind and help calm the other dogs down," she said, twisting a braid around one finger.

I nodded. On the one hand I hated for her to be

scared of Sierra—she'd made so much progress overcoming her fear of big dogs. But until Sierra settled in a bit, it probably made sense for Taylor to focus on the other dogs. And considering Hattie was hidden under her dog bed in her cage, Gus, Humphrey, Daisy, and Popsicle were still huddled in the corner, and Mr. Smashmouth was whimpering a bit, there was plenty to do right here.

I kissed Mr. Smashmouth on his soft head, then handed him over to Taylor. She hugged him close and I could tell it soothed her to have him in her arms. He was great like that. I gave him one last pat, then headed out back with Kim.

The backyard was a pretty perfect dog play area. It was big, with a couple of bushes and one big oak tree to run around. There was a wooden fence along the edge of the property to keep the dogs safe and lots of room for fetch, chase, or a spirited game of tug-of-war.

The air was cool on my face as we walked outside and I breathed in the crisp fall scent. The leaves on the big oak were changing and a few crimson and yellow ones were already on the ground. Soon there would be enough to rake into a pile, which would be fun: the dogs would love jumping on them.

I expected the dogs to be running around but the yard was still, which seemed like a good thing until I realized what they were doing: digging a hole near the fence at the back of the property. Sierra's paws churned out dirt furiously. Boxer was next to her, Lily and Coco on the other side. They were digging a bit too, though nowhere near as vigorously as Sierra. Tim was heading over and Kim and I joined him.

"Sierra, no," Tim said.

At the sound of his voice Coco, Lily, and Boxer stopped, but Sierra carried on like she hadn't heard a thing.

"Boxer, Coco, Lily come," I called, figuring that getting the other dogs away would help. I looked around for the nearest toy and was pleased to see Boxer's favorite a few feet away under the oak tree. It was a bent, chomped-up green Frisbee that was actually kind of gross. But Boxer adored it, so we'd never consider getting rid of it. I grabbed it and tossed it toward the far corner of the yard, away from the hole. And sure enough, as soon as Boxer saw it take off, he rushed after it, Coco and Lily on his heels.

Okay, one problem down, one more to go. Because Sierra was still digging and if she didn't stop soon, she was going to dig her way out of the yard. And Sierra running loose around Roxbury Park would be bad, really bad.

"Let's distract her," Kim said, walking over to a pile of toys in a bin on the porch. She grabbed a bright red rubber ball and I picked up a twisty blue rubber tug toy.

"She has to go for one of these," I said.

We marched over to Sierra and both called her name. The big dog glanced back, then hesitated when she saw what we had in our hands. Kim threw the ball as hard as she could and it bounced off the back porch, then zipped across the yard. Sierra paused, then sprinted after it.

"Well done," Tim said, sounding relieved. "I think we were looking at a jailbreak if we didn't get her to stop soon." Tim sometimes talked in the language of video games, something Kim understood better than I did since she had an older brother. But in this case we were all on the same page: no one wanted to see Sierra escape.

"Let's fill in that hole while we can," I said.

"I'll grab a shovel," Tim said. "I think there's one in the garage. I'll be back in a minute." Then he turned. "Are you guys okay alone? I mean, I know you're great with dogs, but Alice wasn't kidding: Sierra really is a handful."

Tim had never asked anything like that before. But then again, we'd never dealt with a dog like Sierra before. It was nice he was concerned but I knew we were good. "We're fine, thanks," I said.

Tim headed to the side gate while Kim and I walked toward Sierra, who was jogging around with the ball in her mouth. When she saw us coming, she ran over, dropped the ball at Kim's feet, then leaped up putting her front paws on Kim's shoulders, nearly toppling her over.

I reached out and grabbed Kim's arm to brace her.

"Sierra, down," Kim said, calmly and very firmly.

Sierra responded by giving her a kiss on the nose. Which was actually pretty cute, but still, bad dog manners could not be tolerated. And jumping up on someone's shoulders was pretty bad.

"Sierra, down," Kim repeated, even more firmly.

"Should I just take her off you?" I asked.

"No," Kim said, her eyes on Sierra. She was clearly in the dog whisperer zone. "She needs to learn to listen."

It took four more tries but finally Sierra dropped her paws back to the ground and sat at Kim's feet looking up at her. I wasn't sure if Sierra had finally listened or just gotten tired of having her paws up and was ready to play something else. But hopefully she was learning to listen.

Kim picked up the ball and threw it, and Sierra took off. Boxer came over a moment later with his Frisbee, Coco and Lily trotting after him.

"Should we try to get everyone playing together?" I asked Kim.

She shook her head. "Let's give Sierra some one-on-one time. I'll go to the other side of the yard and play with her there."

So that was what we did. I tossed the Frisbee for the three dogs, always careful to keep it away from wherever Sierra was running. And Kim played fetch with Sierra. Sierra made her work for it, dropping the ball, then snatching it up when Kim got close so that Kim would chase her. Whenever the game slowed too much, Sierra bounded back to her hole.

"Found it," Tim called, finally walking back into the yard with the shovel. "Sorry to take so long. It was hidden behind a bunch of stuff."

The sun was sinking toward the horizon, the first hint of a pinky-orange sunset staining the sky. I checked my cell phone and saw that it was almost six o'clock. The Dog Club owners would be here for their dogs any minute.

"Pack that dirt in tight," Kim said, running a hand over her forehead, which was shiny with sweat. "Sierra's very determined to keep working on it."

"Not on my watch," Tim told Sierra, who was edging toward the hole. Then he looked at Kim and grinned. "You got a workout today."

Kim laughed. "I'll say. Next time I'm wearing my gym clothes to Dog Club."

"We'll have to take turns running out this girl's energy," Tim said, pausing in his shoveling to give Sierra a pat on the scruff of her neck. She wagged her tail, then took off after a squirrel that had made the mistake of coming down off the oak tree. It beat a hasty retreat as Sierra galloped over.

The back door opened and Mr. Finnegan came out on the porch. He'd managed to wash the dirty paw prints off his clothes but there were wet patches where the suit material was still drying. I hoped he hadn't gotten in trouble at work for coming back so messy.

"How was she?" he asked. The club dog owners always asked this question, though usually with excitement in their voices. Mr. Finnegan asked with dread.

"She had some wild moments, but we handled them," Kim said. She sounded tired, not in a way that Mr. Finnegan or Tim would notice, but I knew Kim like I knew myself and I could hear an extra softness in her voice. Tim was right—we would definitely have to take turns with Sierra, at least until she settled in.

Sierra had caught sight of her owner and bounded up the porch steps, jumping up with her paws right in his stomach.

Mr. Finnegan grunted and almost fell over. Sierra sat down and looked at him happily, tongue hanging out of her mouth. Two fresh, muddy paw prints decorated the front pockets of Mr. Finnegan's suit.

"Sorry about that," Kim said as she and I headed up the porch stairs.

Mr. Finnegan shook his head ruefully. "This suit was headed to the dry cleaner anyway. These days they're making a mint off of us."

Tim stayed out back with Boxer, Coco, and Lily, so I was hoping that Sierra's exit from the shelter would be a little less dramatic than her entrance had been.

No such luck. Sierra grabbed the ball that Taylor had been using to play fetch with Gus and Hattie, and began her wild romp around the room, a gleam in her eye as though she dared any of the other dogs to try and catch her. None of them did. Hattie took off for her cage; Daisy hid behind Kim; Popsicle, Gus, and Humphrey skidded into a far corner; and Mr. Smashmouth ran right over to me, whimpering. I picked him up and covered his head with kisses to soothe him.

"Sierra, come," Mr. Finnegan said, holding up a dog treat. Sierra's leash was in his other hand. He'd clearly done this before.

Sierra ran over for her treat but as soon as she'd gotten it, she ducked her head away from the leash and took off across the room.

"Do you have another one of those?" Kim asked, going over to Mr. Finnegan.

"Yes," he said. "I come prepared. Sometimes we go through half a box just getting her to come back inside after her morning walk."

"We won't need half a box this time," Kim said determinedly. "You give her the treat and I'll put on her leash."

Mr. Finnegan handed over the thick red leash and called Sierra over again, treat held high. It took two tries but finally Sierra had on her leash and the two of them headed out.

"See you next time," Mr. Finnegan called.

As soon as he'd left Caley drew an arm across her brow in exaggerated relief. "Phew," she said. "That dog is really something."

Taylor, who I hadn't even seen because she'd been half hiding in Alice's office, came out shaking her head. "We have a lot to write in the Dog Club notebook tonight," she said. The club notebook was where we made notes on the dogs we took care of, so we would remember the little things, like their favorite toys, things that scared them, and anything they had trouble with. For Sierra that was going to be a lot!

"Maybe we should hold off doing an entry on her till we see how she settles in," Kim said. She was leaning against a wall and slid down so that she was sitting. "And I think for the Dog Club Diary I'll just talk about how it can take some time for a new dog to adjust."

"But be sure to mention that all the dogs got playtime and attention," I added, ever mindful of wanting to please all our clients. We needed our customers to know that all of the dogs had been cared for. We wanted them to feel confident that their dogs were always in good hands and having fun when they were at Dog Club.

"I didn't get any pictures of Sierra for the post," Taylor said. "I was too busy running for cover."

Caley snorted. "That's not necessarily a bad thing," she said. "We don't want photographic evidence of her running wild around the place."

That was a good point.

"I think I'm ready to go to bed," Kim said with a sigh. Hattie came over and snuggled onto her lap and Kim began petting her.

Caley laughed. "Next time you can stay in with the little dogs," she said. "I'll get my daily workout with Sierra. I need to get in shape for play tryouts anyway." Caley was big into drama and always starred in the high school plays and musicals.

"What play are you guys doing this year?" Taylor asked. She was a lot more relaxed now that Sierra was gone, tossing a tennis ball for Humphrey, Popsicle, and Gus, who had all come out of hiding.

"*A Midsummer Night's Dream*," Caley said. "I want to be Puck."

"Isn't that a boy's part?" Taylor asked. Her dad loved the theater, so she'd seen a lot of shows.

Caley shrugged. "Girls play him too," she said. "And it's the funnest role in the play."

"You'll be awesome then," I said. Mr. Smashmouth was still in my arms, warm and cuddly. I hated that soon I would have to set him down and go home.

But sure enough, a moment later the doorbell rang and the other club dog owners came in.

And after a flurry of furry good-byes, our day at the shelter was over.

"That was quite an afternoon," Taylor said as we headed out into the brisk fall evening. "Alice wasn't kidding about Sierra being a handful."

"You should have seen her digging a hole in the backyard," Kim said, with a chuckle. "We're lucky she didn't make a run for it."

"Yikes," Taylor said. "She really kept you on your toes back there."

"She was sweet too though," I said, thinking of her racing happily after her red ball.

"She was," Kim agreed with a smile. "And I'm sure she'll calm down once she settles into the routine of the club."

"Definitely," I said. Sure, there had been some rough moments. But I knew we'd be okay. Once Sierra got used to the excitement of the shelter and it became part of her regular routine, she would be just fine.

I was sure of it.

4

Do you want your pet to greet you at the door when you come home?

"I'd say yes to that one," Kim said, leaning over my shoulder as the three of us read the quiz I'd bookmarked last night called "Find the Perfect Pet for You." We were in social studies, waiting for the bell to ring, and this was the last question to go before I'd find out what pet was just right for me. The one I would finally be able to convince my mom we had to get.

"What animals greet you at the door though?" Taylor asked, absently twisting a braid around one finger. "Besides dogs obviously."

"Maybe some cats do," Kim said uncertainly.

I frowned. "My mom already said no to dogs and cats, so maybe I should say no."

"I think maybe it's more asking if you want a pet that's friendly," Kim said. "Or the kind that just does its own thing and ignores you."

"Definitely friendly," I said, checking yes, then glancing up to make sure our teacher, Mr. Martin, hadn't noticed my cell phone. He was way nicer than Mrs. Benson but all the teachers gave you a hard time if they saw you with a cell phone. But I just couldn't wait to find out the right pet for me.

The result page came and I read it eagerly. "A rabbit," I announced. Somehow that wasn't exactly what I'd imagined. I was kind of picturing something more active, a pet you could really play with.

"Rabbits are sweet," Taylor said. "Our neighbors in

North Carolina had a hutch in the yard and the rabbits were really cute hopping all over the place. Plus they liked to be held and they were really soft."

That sounded nice.

"They're quiet too," Kim said. "I bet your mom would like that."

"I just need to find out the cleanest way to keep them," I said, starting to get a bit more excited. "So I can really convince my mom." I'd also find out about their care so I could come up with a good argument for how I'd do everything myself, and never forget anything.

The bell rang and I hurriedly hid my cell phone in my pocket as Mr. Martin began passing out our tests on our last unit, the Byzantine Empire. I smiled when I saw mine: an A-minus. It had been a hard test and social studies wasn't my best subject so I knew my mom would be pleased with the grade.

When Mr. Martin set Kim's paper down he stopped to say something to her and I watched her cheeks flush as she sank down in her seat. As soon as he left she stuffed the test into the back of her notebook. Uh-oh. That wasn't good. I knew she'd really studied for the test, but it was tough and it looked like maybe she hadn't done so well. I hoped Mr. Martin would let her do extra credit to make up for it or something. I'd make sure to remind her to ask; sometimes Kim got shy with teachers.

"All right, folks, I know you've been waiting with bated breath to learn what we'll be studying next," Mr. Martin said, rubbing his hands together as though he could barely contain his excitement. Sofia and Jade, who sat next to me, rolled their eyes at each other. It was true Mr. Martin could be pretty over-the-top. I mean, really, who cared about empires from a thousand years ago? But at least he wasn't all crabby about everything like Mrs. Benson.

"The Ottoman Empire!" Mr. Martin exclaimed gleefully. He paused like he was waiting for cheers but needless to say, that didn't happen. Sofia and Jade just rolled their eyes again; Kwan at the desk in front of me was secretly checking something on his phone; and even Carmen, the smartest girl in the class, was just waiting for Mr. Martin to get on with it. "We will not just study this fascinating time in history," he said finally. "We are going to see it, to breathe it, to taste it."

"Did you invent a time machine?" Alec asked from the back row. He always asked questions like that. "Because I'd rather use it to go back to get in with Al Capone and his gang."

His friend Danny reached over to give him a high five.

"A noble goal," Mr. Martin said. "And I suppose you could say that there will be a time machine involved in this unit, but one that you will create. You'll break into small groups and choose a cultural element of the empire, like dance or art or food. Then you'll work to re-create it, and two weeks from today we will have a festival where we will indeed go back in time to experience the life of the Ottomans for ourselves."

Alec was scowling but I thought it sounded pretty

good. Not the work part but the small group part, because that meant working with Kim and Taylor. Taylor was glancing back at me with a grin and we both looked at Kim, who gave us the thumbs-up.

This was going to be fun!

"One more time, my ballerinas," our teacher, Madame Florence, said. "With feeling."

The ten of us in intermediate ballet were dripping sweat after the grueling workout that started with deep stretching, then moved on to barre work and finally ended with the routine we would be doing for our next recital. We'd run through it five times and my calves were burning, my arms ached, and I was panting like I'd just run a race. Which was kind of how I felt. But we all dragged ourselves into our starting positions.

As soon as the music started and I began a series of jetés across the satiny wood floor of the studio, the pain slipped away, replaced by the glorious sensation of flying. I was lost in the music, my body leaping and spinning, light and swift as I glided effortlessly. When I reached my final pose my heart was beating with joy the way it always did when I danced. Sure, my muscles were on fire, but it was so worth it. Nothing felt as good as dance. Except maybe time with the dogs and my friends.

Madame Florence led us through our cooldown and then class was dismissed. I headed for the dressing area, a big room with pale pink walls, posters of Degas's dancers, and rows of lockers against the back wall. I got my stuff out of my locker and then settled on a back bench to take off my ballet slippers.

"That was a hard class," my friend Dana said, sitting down next to me and tugging at the pins holding her black hair up in a tight bun. She went to Roxbury Park Middle School too and our moms often carpooled to dance classes, at least when I didn't forget to tell my mom.

"Tell me about it," our friend Asha groaned. She went to school in the next town over, Millerton, but we'd all been taking dance together for years so we knew each other well. And this year the three of us had been selected for the dance school company, which meant we took three dance classes a week and had solos in the end-of-term performances. Being in the company was fun but a lot of work.

"My feet are going to be sore tonight," I said, shimmying out of my leotard. My mom would be here soon and I didn't want to keep her waiting, not when I was ready to unleash my rabbit plan.

"You should soak them in warm water and Epsom salts," Dana said. "That's what real ballerinas do." Her hair was cascading down her back in shimmering waves. Dana had the best hair, all thick and shiny. I didn't bother taking mine out of my bun because after being tightly coiled for class it would stick out like I'd poked my finger into an electrical socket. I'd just wash it tonight so it was normal for school in the morning.

"I think I'm going to have to soak my whole body," Asha said. Her face was shiny with sweat.

"Sasha, what are you and Kim and Taylor going to do for our social studies project?" Dana asked. She knew who I'd be working with just like I knew she'd be with Emily, Naomi, and Rachel.

"We haven't decided yet," I said. I put my dirty clothes in my bag and pulled on my jeans. "What about you guys?"

"We're probably doing a dance," she said. "So if you guys do too, we should make sure we don't do the same kind."

"Good thinking," I said, taking a quick look at myself in the mirror along one wall of the dressing room and smoothing down a few pieces of hair that had sprung loose from my bun. "I bet they had a lot of dances, so we can just pick different ones." I was definitely going to try and talk Kim and Taylor into a dance—that seemed a lot easier than any of the other options. Though that was probably just because I liked to dance.

"See you guys later," I said, hoisting my dance bag

over my shoulder and walking out to the parking lot.

The sun was setting, the sky streaked with orange and gold, as I headed to my mom's little white Honda, which was, of course, spotless.

"Hi, honey," she said as I slid into the front seat. Not surprisingly it was only this year, when I'd turned twelve, that she let me sit in the front seat. I felt grown-up next to her as she turned the car down Olive Avenue, toward the big grocery store, Old Farm Market, just outside of town. It was in a strip mall, tucked between a dollar store and the place that I was focused on: Paula's Pet Emporium.

"How was your day?" she asked.

"It was good," I said. "I got an A-minus on my social studies test." I knew this would make my mom happy and I wanted her to be in a good mood.

"Nice job," she said, clearly pleased. "You studied a lot and it paid off."

"I did work hard," I said. My mom was really into hard work, so I wanted to emphasize that.

We pulled into the lot at Old Farm Market and my mom grabbed a cart out front. "Want to get eggs and butter while I start in the meat section?" she asked.

"Sounds good," I said. We were always efficient at shopping but I made sure to be extra fast today so that we'd have a little time at the end.

Ten minutes later our cart was filled with everything we needed and my mom headed for the checkout line.

"Can I go to the Pet Emporium while you pay?" I asked, after I'd helped her put everything up on the conveyer belt.

My mom was distracted as she gave our reusable shopping bags to the cashier. "Okay, but be quick."

"Actually I was hoping you could meet me there," I said, looking at her with pleading eyes. "There's something I really want to show you."

My mom sighed but nodded. "Okay, but just for a second. And we aren't buying anything else today."

"Of course not," I said. That was fine. We could

select our rabbit today and then go pick her up over the weekend.

I practically skipped out of the market and over to the Pet Emporium, where I was greeted by the smell of wood shavings and the squeaks and scuffling sounds of a lot of animals. In other words, heaven!

"Can I help you?" the saleswoman asked. She wore cat's-eye glasses, which seemed fitting, and her salt-and-pepper hair hung loose around her shoulders.

"I'd like to meet some of your rabbits," I told her.

"Sure," she said, coming out from behind the counter. "They're just over here." She led me to a glass cage off to one side where four black and white rabbits sat on a thick bed of shredded paper.

Good, my mom would like the paper—no dust.

One rabbit was gnawing on a rubber chew toy and the others were just kind of sitting there. Maybe they were tired. For a second I thought of the dogs at the shelter, especially Mr. Smashmouth, all bouncy and fun. But my mom had said no to a dog, so I needed to focus on what might still be possible, and right now that was a rabbit.

"They're cute," I said. They really were, all soft fluffy fur and feathery ears. My mom was going to love them.

"Can I hold one?" I asked.

"Sure," the saleslady said, taking a key ring out of her pocket and using one to unlock the cage. "Which one?"

I was about to answer when the door of the store opened and my mom came in. She was frowning slightly and there was a crease in her forehead, right between her eyes. I knew this meant she was feeling rushed and wanted to get home.

"Um, that one," I said quickly, pointing at the nearest rabbit, who was mostly white with three black spots on her face. Or his face. It was impossible to tell.

The saleswoman scooped up the rabbit. "Be sure to support his back legs," she said as she handed him to me.

He was lighter than I expected. His fur was silky but I could feel the bones of his back poking against my hand. I shifted it but I still had the poking feeling. Maybe rabbits were just bony.

"Hi," I said to him gently.

He looked at me and blinked, then looked away, his little white nose twitching but otherwise completely still. I wondered if he was scared and he'd be more active once he was home.

"Sash, put that away and let's go," my mom said in her no-nonsense voice as she came up.

"But look how cute he is," I said, resting a cheek against his fur. "Don't you want to pet him?"

My mom shook her head. "No, I don't want to get any fur on my blazer."

"Rabbits don't shed a lot," the saleswoman said. I could have kissed her: it was the best possible thing to say.

"And they're very clean," I said. "Look, their cages just have shredded paper, no dusty wood."

"Lovely," my mom said. "Now give him back and let's get going."

I handed the rabbit back to the saleswoman and

thanked her. My mom had seen the rabbit and hopefully that was enough. She wasn't looking that excited but I was still hoping I could talk her into it on the ride home.

"No," my mom said the second we were in the car.

"No what?" I asked, suddenly worried I'd forgotten something.

"No rabbit," my mom said, putting the key in the ignition and starting the car.

Wait, how had she gotten three steps ahead of my argument?

"But Mom," I began.

She was shaking her head. "No buts," she said. "I know how much you want a pet, but it's not going to happen, not now. A pet is a huge responsibility, one you just aren't ready for."

"I am, Mom, I know I am," I said, trying really hard not to whine.

"Sash, you just don't understand how much work it is to care for a pet," she said. "I know you want to and I know you'd try. But that little rabbit would need food and water and a clean cage and some kind of cleaning every day, no matter how busy you were, no matter what else you needed to do."

"I know that," I started, but my mom held up a hand.

"For the first few weeks it would be fun," she said. "But then it would be boring and take time away from homework and dance and you'd start to resent it."

"I wouldn't, I really wouldn't," I said, clenching my hands together. She didn't understand how much I wanted a pet, how it would be more important than anything else I had going on. If I could just make her understand that—

"You say that now but the truth is, you don't know," she said. "And I do. I've been around a little longer than you and I know stuff like this. When you're older we can talk about it again but for now the answer is no. Period."

There was a hollow feeling in my chest as I sat back in my seat. We were driving along Main Street, the store lights casting a soft glow over the road in front of us. As we passed the shelter I thought of sweet Mr. Smashmouth and my heart twisted. I couldn't wait to get to the shelter the next day and give him a big hug. He would make me feel better, at least while I got to be with him. But then I'd be home again, with no animal to snuggle with. I didn't want to wait for a pet, I wanted one *now.* To wait even a month felt like forever.

As we drove through the quiet night I thought back to what my mom had said. What it all came down to, really, was her thinking I wasn't responsible enough. Nothing I said had convinced her, so maybe it was time to stop *telling* her how responsible I was, and show her.

I felt a flicker of excitement as the idea took hold. Instead of arguing with my mom I'd just stop forgetting things. I'd do everything I was supposed to and more. I'd let her see for herself how responsible I could be when I tried.

And once she saw that, I knew she'd finally let me have a pet!

5

"Ugh, I hate it when they run out of strawberry yogurt," Taylor said with a frown as we stood in line at the school cafeteria. The room was steamy and reeked of boiled cabbage, the side vegetable that came with today's hot meal of beef Stroganoff. The smell alone would put anyone off eating it, but we did have a good salad bar, semidecent sandwiches, and Taylor's favorite, yogurt. Though they always ran out of strawberry first.

"How about blueberry?" Kim asked, pointing to

Taylor's second favorite.

"It'll have to do," Taylor said with a small pout. Then she grinned. "Oh, and my aunt Selena sent me a care package of her famous mini moon pies and I brought us some."

"Yummy," I said as I put some sliced chicken on the salad I was making. Madame Florence encouraged all her dancers to eat a healthy diet, which was why I'd recently started eating salads for lunch. But one little moon pie wouldn't hurt, especially the ones Taylor's aunt Selena made. I'd had them before and they were amazing.

"We just have to finish fast so we can go to the library," Kim said, picking at the chipping pink polish on her thumbnail. She'd already gotten her usual turkey sandwich and put it on her tray. I knew she was eager for us to start researching our social studies project since she'd done so badly on the last test. Taylor and I hurried to pay, and then the three of us headed to our regular table along the back wall near a window.

"Hey, guys," Emily said from the next table as we set our stuff down. One of the nice things about going to a small school was you knew pretty much everyone. Maybe you didn't *like* everyone, but Emily, Dana, Naomi, and Rachel were awesome and excellent cafeteria table neighbors.

"Sash, are your calves aching today?" Lily asked with a grimace. She was eating salad too.

"Totally," I said, unwrapping my fork. I kind of liked the feel of sore muscles though, because I knew it meant they were getting stronger.

"I can't wait to see you guys perform," Kim said. She came to every one of my recitals and cheered as loud as my mom.

"Me either," Taylor said with a grin. "I hear you guys are the best."

"They are," Rachel said. She, Emily, and Naomi always came too. "Wait till you see them."

I felt flush with all the praise and I could see Dana's cheeks were pink too.

"Do you guys want some mini moon pies?" Taylor asked, pulling out a plastic container and passing it to their table. "They're my aunt Selena's specialty."

"Mm, I can see why," Naomi said after taking a bite. "Thanks."

They passed the pies back to us and then turned back to their lunches.

"I'm so glad we get to go to the shelter this afternoon," I said as I dug into my salad. I couldn't wait to cuddle up with Mr. Smashmouth.

"Me either," Taylor agreed as she took the foil top off her yogurt. "I just hope Sierra's a little calmer today." The corners of her mouth turned down slightly and she had a wrinkle in her forehead, both signs that she was feeling anxious. I hated that Sierra's overenergized antics were making Taylor's fears flare up again.

"I bet she will be," I said. "I mean, now she's spent time at the shelter, so it won't all be new." I turned to Kim. "That has to soothe her, at least a little, right?"

But Kim shook her head slowly. "Not necessarily,"

she replied. "I think if she was just excited about the new surroundings she'd have calmed down after being there for a while."

"Oh," I said, feeling a bit deflated.

Kim put a hand on my arm and gave me a reassuring squeeze. "It was a good thought."

I grinned. "That's why you're the dog whisperer," I said. "You know these things."

She ducked her head and her cheeks turned pink.

"And that's why we need you now," Taylor said, running her spoon around the side of her yogurt carton. "We have to figure out some way to get Sierra to stop taking the shelter apart."

"And terrifying the other dogs," I added, picturing poor Mr. Smashmouth and the others cowering in the corner.

"I think taking Sierra outside first thing will help," Kim said. "We just have to make sure she doesn't dig again."

"Do you think she can play with the other dogs?"

I asked. "It seems kind of unfair if only she gets to go outside since the other dogs really like it out there too."

"That's a good point," Kim said. "But I'm not sure Sierra can handle fetch with any of the others. Maybe we take her out alone for the first fifteen minutes and then see how she does with some of the others?"

"Sounds worth trying," I said, taking a big bite of my salad. The cafeteria had filled up since we'd arrived and all around us kids laughed and talked, creating a cheerful din. I liked all the energy of everyone being together—it was one of the things that made lunch fun.

But Kim was stuffing the last of her sandwich into her mouth and standing up. "You guys ready?" she asked as soon as she'd swallowed.

I hurriedly ate the last of my salad as Taylor passed around the plastic container of moon pies. I took a small one and bit into it as I gathered my things. Rich chocolate and smooth cream—totally divine!

I finished it as we dumped our trash and headed to the big doors at the front of the cafeteria. I almost tripped over Henry Mattox's backpack because I was so busy enjoying my pie. But Taylor grabbed my elbow before I could fall.

"Thanks," I said.

"Anytime," she said with a grin, then pushed open the door.

The hall was so quiet after the cafeteria that it seemed almost eerie as we walked to the library.

"It's like a scene from a horror movie," Kim said, thinking the same thing as me, like always.

"The girls felt perfectly safe as they walked the familiar halls of their school," Taylor said in a spooky voice. "They had no idea that Axel the ax killer was roaming the hall behind them, just waiting for another innocent victim. Or three."

The three of us cracked up. We were still laughing when we walked into the library. Some librarians might insist on complete quiet but Ms. Cho said books should make you laugh out loud or gasp in surprise, so a little noise in her library was approved of.

She was at her desk scanning in books and she smiled as we came up. "How can I help you ladies today?" she asked.

"We're doing a social studies project on the Ottoman Empire," Kim said, the laughter gone from her face as she got down to business.

"For Mr. Martin's class, right?" Ms. Cho asked.

We nodded.

"Let me show you where we keep those books," she said, standing up. "And I can give you a list of online resources if you need them."

"Perfect," I said.

The library was a big room lined with tall bookcases along the walls and down the middle of the room. There were sturdy wooden tables between the rows where years of Roxbury Park Middle School students before us had carved their names. Kim had actually found a table where her dad had scratched out his initials and she really liked teasing him about defacing property. I knew if my mom had grown up here, she'd never have done anything like that. My grandparents said that even when she was a kid she cared about keeping things neat.

"Here we go," Ms. Cho said, stopping at a shelf near the back of the room. "These are all the books we have on the Ottomans. I'll leave you to it and let me know if you need anything."

We thanked her and then started looking through the titles, pulling down a bunch of books to help get us started. We brought our pile to the nearest table and began flipping through them.

"This empire was around for ages," Taylor said as she skimmed a few pages. "Literally hundreds of years."

"That should give us a lot to choose from," I said. I noticed Kim was twisting a lock of hair tightly around her fingers as she read through the table of contents in her book. "We'll find something so great it will knock Mr. Martin's socks off." Kim's dad always said corny things like "knock your socks off" and they always made her smile.

Sure enough, she grinned. "I hope so," she said. "I

need a grade that's so high it knocks my parents' socks off."

"That's the goal then," Taylor said. "All socks knocked off."

We were quiet for a moment as we looked through our books.

"They had some pretty cool art," Taylor said, showing us a picture with beautiful calligraphy and an etching of birds. "Maybe we could copy some of it and write about what it means?"

"That sounds really hard," Kim said anxiously.

I went back to my book, which was about culture in the Ottoman Empire. "It says here that dance was important, especially belly dancing," I said after a moment, picturing us in spangly outfits. "That could be fun."

But now Kim was looking queasy. "There's no way I can do a dance in front of our whole class," she said.

"Actually I think the festival will be for the whole

grade," Taylor said.

Kim grimaced. "Even worse." She looked at me guiltily. "Sorry, Sash."

"Don't worry," I said. I'd had a feeling she wouldn't want to do it. Honestly I wasn't sure I wanted to show my belly to the whole grade anyway. "We'll find something else even better."

A group of eighth graders sat down at the table next to us and began talking in low voices.

"The Ottomans had some epic poems," Taylor said. "Maybe we could recite one."

"I don't think we'd get a good grade for just reading a poem," Kim said.

She was really tense about this project!

"Well, we could research the poet and say something about the role of poetry or something," Taylor said patiently.

"I'm worried that's not special enough," Kim said.

Taylor shot me a look that clearly said "help."

"Um, what if we cook something?" I asked. I had

just gotten to the section in my book about meals. "I bet they had a lot of special dishes."

Kim was finally nodding at something. "That could be good," she said. "And then we can write about their dining customs."

"Mr. Martin will love it," Taylor said. Then she grinned. "I vote we make something sweet."

"I second that," I said.

We began flipping through pages again, searching out desserts.

"What about candied chestnuts?" I asked.

Kim shook her head. "Not fancy enough."

"I've got it," Taylor said excitedly. "Turkish delight!"

Kim beamed. "That's perfect!" Then she scrunched her eyebrows again. "But what is it?"

"It's a candy," Taylor said, looking back down at her book. "It looks like it's soft, like gumdrops. And you can make it with different flavors, like orange or rose."

I wrinkled my nose. "Rose candy doesn't sound so good."

"But it would be authentic," Kim said. She had

gotten up and was reading over Taylor's shoulder. "We want it to be just like they did it back then."

"Okay," I said. Maybe it would be tasty.

"It sounds kind of messy to make," Taylor said after she'd read through the recipe.

Kim shot me a grin. "We won't be making it at your house," she said. "Remember that time we baked cookies and forgot to wipe the flour off the counter? Your mom was so not happy."

"Yeah, that was bad," I said, thinking of my mom's scowl that day and then remembering my vow to show her how responsible I actually was. Choosing not to do something messy in her kitchen seemed like a good first step.

"We can do it at my house," Taylor said. "There's always a mess in our kitchen, the way Anna cooks."

Taylor's mom had died when she was little so she and her sisters all did work around the house to keep things running smoothly. Her bossy older sister Anna had the job of making their dinner during the week. When Taylor was first learning how to make big dogs at the shelter obey her, Kim advised her to use the bossiest tone she knew, so Taylor imagined she was talking to her older sister Anna. It worked like a charm.

The bell was about to ring so we closed up our books and put them back on the shelf. Then we headed out.

"Our project is going to be great," Taylor said. "Everyone's going to love eating candy in school." Roxbury Park Middle School had a no-candy rule, so Taylor was definitely right about that.

"I just hope Mr. Martin likes it too," Kim said worriedly.

I put an arm around her shoulders. "He will," I promised.

Taylor slung an arm around Kim from the other side. "And we'll get an A," she predicted.

All three of us were smiling as we headed down the hall together.

6

"Whoops, can someone grab that leash?" Mr. Finnegan asked. But it was too late. He'd just walked into the shelter with Sierra, who took one look at Hattie, Gus, and Popsicle playing fetch with Taylor and thundered over. Her leash was still clipped to her collar and it flew out behind her, almost hitting Gus in the face as Sierra lunged for the tennis ball the other dogs had been chasing.

"Someone better grab that leash before one of the

dogs gets hurt," Tim said. He had his hands full with Boxer, who was riled up by Sierra's grand entrance and was jumping up on him.

I wanted to help but I was holding Mr. Smashmouth, who burrowed into my arms as Sierra's nails scraped along the floor. He was too frightened for me to just put him down.

Taylor was closest to Sierra and I could see her shrink back a bit. But then she took a deep breath. "Sierra, heel," she said in a clear, strong Anna voice.

I was so proud of her!

But unfortunately Sierra took no notice. Instead she grabbed the tennis ball in her mouth and began racing around the shelter, leash still flapping behind her. Taylor flattened herself against the wall, eyes wide, as Sierra tore past.

"I'm so sorry about this," Mr. Finnegan said, looking helpless as the smaller dogs fled for their cages.

"We can handle it," Kim said in a confident voice, but I could see her frowning, which was not a good sign. Still, when Sierra came close, Kim moved directly in front of her and said, "Sierra, heel," in the firmest voice ever.

Sierra tried to duck past but Kim had slowed her down and was able to grab her collar. "Heel," Kim said, pulling up Sierra's leash and holding it tight.

And Sierra finally came to a halt.

"Bravo," Caley cheered.

"Yes, that was well done," Mr. Finnegan said. He sounded tired and he had a few leaves in his hair, as though he'd been dragged through a bush. Which, knowing Sierra, seemed very possible. "I'll just leave her with you then," he said. "Thank you so much. She does have a lovely time here." With that he was gone.

"I wouldn't use the word 'lovely,'" Caley said as Sierra lunged forward, nearly pulling Kim over. "Insanely wild maybe. Or utterly riotous."

Those *were* better words.

The shelter had been cheerfully energetic before Sierra's arrival, with Mr. Smashmouth running up to greet me first thing and the other shelter dogs eager to say hi to us and the club dogs we came in with. Humphrey was happily gnawing on a rawhide bone he found, while Boxer and Lily began romping around with Coco. Tim and Caley were playing fetch with Daisy and Alice was out running errands. It had been another perfect afternoon, at least until Sierra burst in.

Now it was time to figure out how to make things perfect *with* Sierra. I knew there had to be a way and I was certain we'd come up with something good. Already the smaller dogs were cautiously coming out of their cages. Maybe they were getting more comfortable with Sierra's big energy. Mr. Smashmouth seemed most comfortable in my arms, though, so I kept him there. I was happiest snuggling him anyway.

"Okay, I'm going to take Sierra's leash off now," Kim said. "Everybody ready?"

I noticed Taylor getting as far as she could from Sierra while the rest of us braced ourselves. Which was smart because the second the leash was off, Sierra surged forward, rushing at Hattie, who had just picked up the tennis ball in her mouth.

Hattie yipped in terror as Sierra charged, and the ball rolled away. Sierra changed course to follow it while Hattie raced over to Taylor, yipping the whole way. Taylor bent down and began to soothe her, talking to her gently and petting her. The other dogs meanwhile ran for cover while Mr. Smashmouth pressed himself even closer to me. And not surprisingly there was no sign of Oscar. We wouldn't see him again until Sierra was long gone.

"Do you think it's time for Sierra to go outside for a bit?" I called to Kim over the crash of Sierra hitting Lily's cage as she raced around the room.

How was it that the shelter felt big and roomy until Sierra got here? Now it felt cramped and tiny, despite the fact only one dog was running around. At least until Boxer got in on the action and began chasing Sierra.

"That's not going anywhere good," Tim said, trying to distract Boxer with his favorite Frisbee.

Kim had heard my question and was already herding Sierra out.

"Are you guys okay if I go with Kim and Sierra?" I asked, reluctantly setting Mr. Smashmouth down.

"We're fine," Caley said. "See what you guys can do to calm her down a bit."

By the time I got to the backyard Sierra was already streaking to the far corner, paws churning as she went.

"Let's let her run out some of this energy," Kim said. It was a warm day with the smell of leaves and sunshine perfuming the air and it was invigorating to be out in the pretty backyard, even if my arms did feel a bit cold without Mr. Smashmouth.

Sierra spent about five minutes running in wild circles, then she headed over to her digging spot from the previous day. But this time we were ahead of her.

"Sierra," I called, holding up a blue rubber ball. As soon as she looked back I tossed it for her, in the opposite direction of the hole. Then I breathed a sigh of relief when Sierra chased after it.

We played with her for another ten minutes and then Kim suggested we take her back inside. "Let's see if this helped," she said. "Because we can't spend every afternoon at the shelter outside with Sierra."

She was right. It wasn't fair to the other dogs or to Alice, Caley, Tim, and Taylor. And as fun as it was to play fetch with Sierra, I missed my time with the other dogs.

Sierra flew up the porch steps.

"Sit," Kim told her when she began to scratch at the door.

Sierra looked up at Kim as though she was asking, "Do I really have to?"

"Sit," Kim repeated.

Sierra wagged her tail.

"Sit," Kim repeated. Clearly she was willing to do this all day until Sierra listened. Which was one of the many things that made Kim so good with dogs.

I guess Sierra figured that out too because she finally sat. Kim rewarded her with a dog treat she'd stuck in her pocket, then opened the door for Sierra.

Sierra dashed in like she'd been locked up for hours.

"That didn't work so well, did it," Kim said glumly as we watched the smaller dogs race for their cages yet again.

"I'll take her for a walk," Caley said.

It took all of us to corner Sierra and stop her long enough to snap the leash onto her collar. Then she galloped for the door, pulling Caley after her.

"Good luck," I called as they headed out. The second the coast was clear Mr. Smashmouth darted over to me and I scooped him up.

"Yikes," Taylor said, wiping her hand across her forehead in an exaggerated gesture. "That was rough."

"I'll say," Kim said with a sigh. Hattie and Gus ran over to her and she began to pet them. Lily joined in and soon Kim was down on the floor with all three dogs on her lap. She looked blissfully happy.

I felt the same, now that I had Mr. Smashmouth back in my arms.

"I think we have a problem with Sierra," Tim said. He was playing catch with Boxer and Popsicle but his normal smile was gone and he looked serious. "Taking her outside to calm down isn't working."

"It's not," Kim agreed heavily.

"We'll just have to figure something else out," I said. I put Mr. Smashmouth down so he could get some exercise, and picked up a small blue and white striped ball to throw for him. He was nearly blind but you'd never know it watching him race around after that toy. He was so cute!

"Maybe a long walk will help," Taylor said. She was sitting on the floor near Kim playing a gentle game of tug-of-war with Coco.

"Doesn't she get a walk when Mr. Finnegan brings her here?" Tim asked. Boxer came up and dropped his Frisbee at Tim's feet, then did a little dance of excitement as Tim picked it up and threw it again.

"Actually I think they live pretty close," Kim said, sounding more hopeful again. You could barely see her under all three dogs. "So she isn't out that much before she gets here. It might help if one of us took her out for a long walk first thing."

"Maybe to the park where she could run around too," Taylor said. "Not that I'm volunteering to do it of course. Sierra is out of my league."

"I think she might be out of all our leagues," Tim muttered.

I was positive he was wrong. We just had to figure out the secret of calming Sierra and once we had that, everything would be fine. Great, even.

"So we'll try a long walk and see if that helps," Kim said cheerfully. I knew she believed we could make it work too.

Mr. Smashmouth dropped his ball at my feet and wagged his tail. "You're so clever," I told him, rubbing his soft little head before throwing the ball for him again. There was something wonderful about playing catch with a dog, the rhythm of it maybe, or the way the dog was thrilled every single time you tossed the ball. Whatever it was, I felt like I could do it forever.

"Let me show you guys some of the pictures I took for the blog," Taylor said, bringing her camera over to Kim. I headed over too, carrying the ball so Mr. Smashmouth and I could keep up with our game. Taylor took great photos and I loved seeing our time with the dogs documented.

The first picture was of Hattie, Lily, and Boxer all leaping up to grab a red Frisbee.

"Too cute!" I squealed.

The next one showed Popsicle, Gus, and Daisy playing fetch with Tim; then there was one of Coco and Mr. Smashmouth on the floor with a tug-of-war toy. Next was a shot of Humphrey with a blue ball in his mouth.

"I like that one," Kim said as Taylor clicked to a new photo. It was a picture of me holding Mr. Smashmouth. He was nuzzling close and my cheek was pressed against his soft fur.

"I like that one too," I said softly. It was funny to

see how happy I looked holding Mr. Smashmouth. I mean, I knew I *felt* happy, of course. But seeing it was different—it was like my whole face was glowing.

"I wish we could post it but I'll send it to you," Taylor said. Our parents didn't let us put photos of ourselves on the blog, just ones of the dogs. "And we can use the one of the dogs playing Frisbee on today's entry."

"The one of Humphrey too," I said. "And Coco and Mr. Smashmouth. They're all such good pictures!"

"Oh, but not this one," Taylor said. She had just moved on to the next photo and it was clearly an accidental shot because it was so blurry. But you could still make out Sierra bearing down on Popsicle, Gus, and Hattie, the little dogs racing away, a manic gleam in Sierra's eyes.

"Yikes, we definitely don't want the club dog owners seeing that," I agreed.

"It's gone," Taylor said, deleting it.

"I'm thinking maybe we don't write about it in the blog either," I said. Mr. Smashmouth dropped his ball at my feet and wagged his tail. I stroked his ears for a moment before throwing the ball again. "I mean, we don't want the other owners to be worried about their dogs when they're here." When my mom opened her own law firm a few years ago she'd talked a lot about needing good word of mouth, especially when you first start a business, so I knew how much it mattered. We needed the club dog owners raving about us to their friends, not stressing about a big dog scaring everyone.

Hattie brought Kim a tennis ball that she threw gently across the room. "We don't want to lie though," she said. Hattie, Gus, and Lily darted after the bouncing ball and Popsicle came running over to join them.

"That's true," Taylor agreed. "But we don't go into everything on the blog anyway. Maybe we just mention the new dog is still a little, ah, rambunctious."

"And also say we know she'll settle in soon," I added. Mr. Smashmouth was back and this time I picked him up for a hug. He rewarded me with a big kiss on the cheek. "Are there any good pictures of her, in case the

Finnegans look on the website?"

Taylor scrolled through her camera and then shook her head. "I'll try to get one next time," she said. "I bet the walk will help and she'll have a few quiet moments I can capture."

Kim nodded. "Okay, sounds good."

It did sound good. And maybe the long walk first thing would be the answer. Then Sierra could settle into the club and everything would be perfect again.

7

"Yuck, what is that smell?" Kim asked as the three of us walked into the cafeteria. There was already a line of kids at the salad and sandwich bar, but just a few people were waiting for the hot lunch option, which smelled a bit like boiled gym socks. We skipped it and headed straight for salad and sandwiches.

Kim grabbed a turkey sandwich and a Baggie of baby carrots while I picked up the tongs and began setting a bed of lettuce on my plate.

"Ooh, the last one," Taylor said, reaching excitedly for the one remaining container of strawberry yogurt.

But just then someone's hand shot out and grabbed the yogurt from Taylor's grasp.

"Hey," I said indignantly, dropping the tongs and turning around.

The girl who had taken the yogurt ignored me. She was busy looking at Taylor, a small smile playing around the corners of her mouth. Her name was Brianna and she had moved to Roxbury Park a year ago. We'd never been in the same class, so I didn't really know her, but I'd never seen her do anything obnoxious, at least not until right now.

"You don't mind, do you?" Brianna asked Taylor. Her voice sounded almost like a dare.

I waited for Taylor to unleash some of her famous Southern attitude on Brianna, maybe even using the Anna voice, but to my surprise Taylor just dropped her eyes. "No problem," she said.

"Thanks, new girl," Brianna said triumphantly as

she strode off with two of her friends.

"Taylor, that was yours," I said indignantly.

"She totally just grabbed it from you," Kim agreed.

Taylor shrugged. "It's no big deal," she said.

Maybe not but it still annoyed me. "Do you have classes with her?" I asked as I added tomato slices to my salad.

"She's in my science class," Taylor said, picking up a blueberry yogurt. "And she's just one of those people, you know? Like if she doesn't get what she wants she makes a big thing of it. It's easiest to leave her alone."

I wasn't sure about that, but then Taylor was the one with three older sisters, so she probably knew more about when to argue and when to let things go.

We wove our way through the crowded cafeteria and sat down at our table. Emily, Dana, Rachel, and Naomi waved but they were busy talking about their social studies project, which was exactly what we were planning to do too.

"Okay, so we know we're making Turkish delight

for the festival," Kim said. Instead of unwrapping her sandwich she began tapping her fingers on top of it. "I can do some research about it, like who first created it and how it was served and stuff."

"Sounds good," Taylor said, dipping her spoon into her yogurt. "I can look up facts about the cuisine during the Ottoman Empire, and Sash, maybe you can read about dining customs."

"Perfect," I said. "I think that's more than enough to get us an A."

"We just have to make sure we do a really good write-up," Kim said quickly. "And that we document our research."

It made my chest ache to hear how tense she sounded.

"We totally will," I said, smiling at her. "We're going to ace this assignment."

Kim bit her lip but then she nodded and finally began eating.

"We do need to do at least one practice run of

cooking the Turkish delight," Taylor said. She'd dribbled some yogurt on her tray and was wiping it up with a napkin. Which made me think of cooking messes. And all of a sudden, something occurred to me.

"You guys, let's cook it at my house," I said, thinking it through as I spoke. If we cooked at Taylor's my mom would never know I'd done something responsible, not unless I told her about it. And cooking it at someone else's house wasn't exactly impressive. However, my mom coming home to a sparkling clean kitchen and being presented with the complicated project we'd concocted in that very same kitchen? *That* was impressive. The kind of impressive that might open her mind to the possibility of a pet.

"Wait, why?" Kim asked in surprise. "I thought you didn't want to mess up your kitchen."

"We don't want to get you in trouble with your mom," Taylor added.

I didn't want to get into how my mom thought I was still a little kid who couldn't take care of stuff. "I just think we can handle it, you know?" I said. "There aren't even that many ingredients in Turkish delight and we have a really nice kitchen. We should use it."

"Our stove does have a problem with burning things," Taylor said. "My dad is going to get a new one but who knows how long that will take."

"My parents wouldn't mind if we did it at my house," Kim said. "But they have that rule about me not using the stove when they're out, so we couldn't do it until the weekend."

It was funny how parents were strict in different ways. Like Kim's family preferred her to hang out at the diner, not be home alone when they were working long hours at the family business. And they monitored her homework time really carefully. My mom didn't do any of that and she needed me to use the stove before she got home so we could have dinner ready before my bedtime. But then Kim's family didn't care about messes or do room inspections for cleanliness like my mom. And I knew they thought Kim was responsible.

At least in this case though, the rules worked perfectly for what I was planning.

"So we'll do it at my house, no problem," I said.

A balled-up napkin came flying over and landed smack in the middle of our table. "Ew," Kim said as we all pulled our food away from it.

We looked to see where it had come from. Two tables down Dennis, Jonah, and Silas were having a food fight and the cafeteria aides were rushing over.

"Why are boys so immature?" Taylor asked. "Food fights are so fifth grade."

"Seriously," I agreed. I took my last bite of salad but I was still a little hungry. I wished Taylor had brought mini moon pies again.

"Want some carrots?" Kim asked, pulling open the little bag she'd bought and reading my mind.

"Thanks," I said, grabbing two.

"Hey, speaking of carrots, how did it go when you asked your mom for the rabbit?" Taylor asked with a grin.

I wrinkled my nose and shook my head. "It was a no-go."

"Oh, too bad," Kim said sympathetically.

"Actually it's okay," I said. "When we went to the Pet Emporium and I held one of their rabbits it didn't feel quite right. Like, he was cute and everything, but it didn't feel like it was a fit for me."

"I guess that means more pet quizzes," Kim said, holding up the bag to offer me more carrots.

"Yes," I said, helping myself to another. "Eventually I'm going to figure out the perfect pet, the one that my mom cannot say no to."

"I have an idea for you," Taylor said, her eyes sparkling. She was done with her yogurt and she grabbed a carrot too. "It's an animal that gets a bad rap but really they're super smart and clean, even though they like garbage."

"This sounds like the start of a bad joke," I said.

Kim nodded, grinning.

"Okay, tell me," I said to Taylor.

"A pig!" she cried happily.

The thought of my mom ever allowing a pig into our house was too much—we all burst out laughing. We were still giggling when the bell rang.

That night I took special care to do everything my mom had asked in the text she sent me that afternoon. I started the pasta water before she got home, I took the sauce she'd made over the weekend out of the freezer to thaw, and I even remembered to get the salad ready. As a bonus I set the table and I was getting our drinks ready when she opened the door. Opened the door to a perfectly clean front hall, I might add: I'd put my shoes on the shoe shelf, my jacket in the closet, and my backpack upstairs in my room. There had been a minor problem with a pile of dirty clothes I needed to wash but I'd stuffed them under my bed. My mom rarely looked there unless she was doing a weekend room inspection. So as far as she was concerned, the house was perfect!

"Thanks for getting everything ready, hon," she

said as we sat down to ravioli with meat sauce and freshly tossed salad. Some families might eat dinner in the kitchen if it was only two people, but not us. We sat in our formal dining room every night, with cloth napkins on the antique oak table, under the chandelier with crystals that sent light dancing around the room.

"No problem," I said casually. I'd decided that part of being responsible was acting like it was no big deal.

"So how as your day?" she asked.

"Good," I said. "I got a one hundred on my English quiz." Mrs. Benson gave surprise pop quizzes at least once a week and by now I knew to always be prepared for one, just in case.

"Nice job," my mom said.

"And Kim and Taylor and I are planning our social studies project," I said. "We came up with something really good." I debated telling her about it but decided it would be most impressive if it was a surprise.

"Do I get to hear about it now or later?" my mom asked, taking a bite of ravioli.

"Later," I said. "We're still figuring out details."

"Sounds like you're putting some hard work into it, which is great," my mom said.

"We're trying," I said, wanting to sound modest but also to make it clear how responsible we were being. "How's work?"

My mom's law firm specialized in environmental law. My mom was really into saving the environment, which was why we never drank bottled water or used plastic grocery bags or paper napkins. She didn't go nuts about it though, like some of her coworkers. There was this one guy who had an outhouse instead of a real toilet, which was totally gross. Most of her job was doing research and writing up briefs, which were basically long, boring essays. But I nodded as she told me about the one she was writing for a case about preserving some forestland outside of town.

"How are things at the dog shelter?" she asked when she was done. "And with the Dog Club?" My mom had been very supportive when we first started the club—she was big on things that helped people and animals, as long as none of it made a mess in our home.

"Pretty good," I said. "Though we have a bit of a challenge with one of the dogs."

"Oh?" She raised an eyebrow as she waited for me to continue.

"It's this new dog, Sierra," I said, pushing my last piece of ravioli along the bottom of my plate to get up the remaining sauce. "She's really energetic and she kind of intimidates the other dogs."

"What kind of dog is she?" My mom took her last sip of seltzer.

"A German shepherd mix," I said.

"That does sound intimidating," my mom said. "Are the owners helpful?"

"Actually I think she kind of intimidates them too," I said, thinking of how bewildered Mr. Finnegan looked when he dropped Sierra off.

"That sounds like a problem," my mom said.

"Yeah, but we're figuring it out," I said eagerly,

realizing this was another way to show how grounded and not flighty I was. "We've been brainstorming ideas to help calm Sierra down so she can play with the other dogs."

"Great," my mom said, smiling. "I'm sure you guys will come up with something good."

"Me too," I said, pleased by her reaction.

We cleared the table together and loaded the dishwasher, and then my mom began to fill the sink to wash the pans she'd used to cook. We put dishes and silverware in the dishwasher but my mom always cleaned the pots by hand.

"Mom, I'll wash up today," I said.

My mom looked confused. "Really?"

Not exactly the reaction I was hoping for. But then again, I'd never offered to wash before. I usually just went up to start my homework.

"Yeah," I said. "You go relax."

My mom gave me a kiss on the head. "What a sweet offer," she said. "Thank you."

I wanted to add that it was responsible as well as sweet but that would be too heavy-handed. Instead I put the colander into the sudsy sink and began to scrub. I washed carefully, making sure every inch of the colander was soaped up before I rinsed and went on to the pasta pot. It took me fifteen minutes to wash three pots but they were super clean and I was proud of them. I headed upstairs thinking I would have to find time for a pet quiz in the next day or two. As responsible as I was being, it was just a matter of time before my mom decided I was ready for a pet.

But an hour later when I came downstairs for a study snack, I heard water running in the sink. I walked in and was horrified to discover my mom rewashing every pot I'd cleaned!

"Mom, I washed those," I said.

My mom looked at me guiltily. "And you did a great job," she said. "I just wanted to give them a quick once-over."

The job couldn't have been that great if they'd

needed a once-over. I wasn't even hungry for my snack anymore. Instead I headed back upstairs, determined to find other ways to prove to my mom that my flighty ways were behind me.

8

"Hey, Sasha," Sofia said as she slipped into her seat at the desk in front of me. The warning bell had just rung and social studies was about to start. "How's it going?"

"Pretty good," I said. "I love your sweater." Sofia and Jade were part of the fashionable group of girls at school—the ones who had been the first to wear makeup and who dressed like models. They always looked nice but also kind of uncomfortable—like her sweater today was woven with glitter thread that was beautiful but also kind of scratchy.

"Thanks," she said, smiling. Some of the girls in their group were a little snobby, but not Sofia or Jade.

The bell rang and Mr. Martin strode to the front of the room. "We'll spend today's class in the library researching your projects on the Ottoman Empire," he announced.

Kim flashed me a smile and I knew she was grateful for the extra time.

"While we're there I'll be coming around to check in, see how everything's going and what kind of help you might need," he said. "Ms. Cho will be on hand as well. So gather up your notebooks and let's go."

I grabbed my stuff and then waited by the classroom door with Kim and Taylor. "What are you doing for the festival?" Carmen asked us.

"We're cooking a kind of candy that they ate during the Ottoman Empire," Taylor told her. "What about you guys?" Carmen was working with Terrell and

Marlena, two of the other kids who got As on everything.

"We're doing what's called a shadow play, with puppets," Carmen said, sounding really excited. It was kind of cool how into school stuff she was. "You know how we learned that the empire was a mix of ethnic groups across a large landmass? There was this famous puppet show called Karagöz and Hacivat that kind of brought together different cultural aspects. We're going to write a report about it and then make puppets and perform it."

I didn't even have to look at Kim to know that her eyes were wide in panic.

"Sounds great," I said calmly.

"All right, people, let's go," Mr. Martin said, opening the door and herding us out into the hall. "Silence until we reach the library, please."

Everyone nodded but as soon as we were out in the hall people began whispering.

"Our project is great," I told Kim before she could

start fretting. "Carmen always does some genius project but everyone else will be doing normal things and ours will be one of the best, I promise."

"But she even knew how to pronounce the name of the puppet show," Kim said. She was picking at her thumbnail as we walked.

"I'm the new girl and even I know that that's typical for Carmen," Taylor said. "I mean, obviously their project will be amazing, but ours will be great too. Totally good enough to knock Mr. Martin's socks off."

Kim managed a small smile at that.

When we got to the library we gathered some books that looked promising and headed to a back table to get to work.

"There was a job called 'imperial food taster' in the Ottoman Empire," Taylor said a few minutes later. "To make sure the food was yummy enough to please the sultan. I'd like that job!"

"Me too," I said.

"Oh, wait, they were also testing for poison, in

case anyone tried to kill the sultan," Taylor said with a frown after she'd read a bit more. "On second thought that wouldn't be the job for me."

"Yikes, me either," I said. "Imagine thinking you could die every time you tried a new dish."

"It's interesting though," Kim said. "It's good information for our report."

"Definitely," Taylor said, noting it down.

"Make sure you write what book it's from," Kim said. "And the page."

I heard Taylor sigh quietly.

"Don't worry, we're doing everything right," I told Kim.

She smiled tiredly. "Sorry, I don't mean to nag."

"We know you're worried, but trust me, it's going to be awesome," Taylor said reassuringly.

Mr. Martin came over to our table. "So what are you ladies working on?" he asked.

Taylor told him about the Turkish delight and he nodded, but then cast a glance at the back table where

Danny and Alec were doing something with rubber bands instead of research.

"Sounds like you have everything in order," he said, a bit distracted as he headed off to the boys.

"He didn't seem that impressed," Kim said, looking after him.

"That's because he had to stop the boys from accidently exploding the library," Taylor said.

We all laughed at that.

"Hi, guys," Dana said as the three of us sat down at our usual lunch table later that day. "What's new?"

"We've taken a trip back in time to the Ottoman Empire," Taylor said, in a spot-on imitation of Mr. Martin that cracked us all up.

"How's your research going?" Emily asked, dipping her spoon into her thermos. She was one of the few people who brought her own lunch to school.

"It's a lot of work," Kim said as she took out her sandwich.

"But we're making good progress," Taylor said, swirling a spoon in her yogurt. "What about you guys?"

"We can't figure out what kind of costumes we should wear for our dance," Naomi said glumly.

"We have a lot of great ideas but they'd all cost way too much," Emily said. "We're trying to figure out what we already have that looks Ottomany."

"I don't think 'Ottomany' is a word," Rachel said, giggling.

"Are you guys belly dancing?" I asked, remembering the bit I'd read about dancing in one of the books on the Ottoman Empire.

The four of them looked horrified. "No way," Naomi said. "Our costumes will definitely be covering our stomachs."

"A wise choice," Taylor said.

After we finished eating I pulled out a book I'd gotten at the library, one that was about animals, just to see if there were any pet ideas I'd overlooked. The first section had pictures and information about fish and other creatures that lived in the water. There were some really colorful fish, and I'd loved *Finding Nemo* when I was a kid, but they seemed like kind of boring pets. I mean, all they did was swim. You couldn't hold them or play with them or anything.

"Do you think your mom would agree to a fish?" Taylor asked, looking over my shoulder.

"It's probably the one thing she'd say yes to right now," I said.

"But you don't want a fish, do you?" Kim asked. She was playing with her sandwich wrapper.

I shook my head. "Not really," I said. "I want a pet I can actually touch." I couldn't help thinking about dogs, but of course that wasn't possible.

"Maybe it's time to consider birds," Taylor said. "You can hold them and they're really pretty colors."

That did sound good. I flipped to the section on birds.

"The parakeets are pretty," Kim said. "Oh, and it says you can teach them tricks. That could be cute."

"And they talk," Taylor said. "Think of all the fun stuff you could teach them to say."

"I'd teach mine to say 'It's Matt's turn to do the dishes,'" Kim said with a grin.

"Mine would say, 'the little sister is the best,'" Taylor said.

Since I had no siblings I couldn't think of anything that fun to teach a bird to say. I mean, "hello" isn't very exciting.

"It says they're social, so that would be good," Kim said.

"It also says they need bird companions, so you should get two," I said, frowning slightly. "My mom won't be as excited about two birds." I wasn't even sure she'd be excited about one.

"But they mate for life," Taylor said, pointing to a paragraph. "How romantic."

"They also need to fly every day," Kim said. "That would be so cool, to have a bird zooming around your house." But then she saw my face. "Oh, but that could get messy, couldn't it."

"Yeah," I said with a sigh. "A bird might not be right after all."

Kim squeezed my shoulder consolingly as the bell rang, but I wasn't all that disappointed. You couldn't really snuggle with a bird after all.

As we gathered up our stuff I decided to take another pet quiz that afternoon at the shelter.

When the final bell rang I got my stuff from my locker, making sure to grab everything I needed. There had been a couple of times I'd forgotten books or notebooks I needed for homework this year, and it always bugged my mom. So now I was taking extra care to have everything I needed. Being responsible was a lot of work, but it would be worth it if I got my pet in the end!

Taylor and Kim were ready to go when I got to Kim's locker, which was our meeting place because her locker was between mine and Taylor's.

"Sorry I'm late," I said, hoisting my backpack over

my shoulder. Being more responsible meant a heavier backpack too.

"Don't worry about it, I just got here too," Taylor said. I had a feeling that wasn't true but it was nice of her to say. My friends never minded my forgetfulness and it was one of the many things I loved about them!

The halls were still full of kids heading home or to after-school clubs, and it was loud. The end of the day was always kind of like a party, with everyone in a good mood. We stuck together as we made our way to the door, dodging a group of boys playing catch with a rolled-up pair of gym socks (no one wanted to get hit by those!) and girls huddled in groups chatting and laughing together.

Just as we turned the corner someone slammed into Taylor from behind, knocking her forward. If Kim hadn't grabbed her elbow she might have fallen.

"Watch it," I said, turning to see who had been so careless. I assumed it was one of the sock boys but it wasn't. It was Brianna carrying a big pile of books.

"Oh, I'm so sorry," she said, not sounding sorry at all. Or maybe that was just how she always sounded? "I didn't see you there."

That was kind of hard to buy: Taylor was pretty tall.

"Don't worry about it," Taylor said, looking slightly shaken up.

"You should look where you're going," I couldn't help telling Brianna.

"I totally will from now on," Brianna said, again sounding pretty fake.

"Are you sure you're okay?" Kim asked Taylor as Brianna took off down the hall.

"I'm fine," Taylor said. "Really, it surprised me but it didn't hurt."

We'd reached the front doors of the school and moved forward into the crowd spilling out on the steps and sidewalk in front of the school. It was a gray day with clouds low in the sky. I hoped it wasn't going to rain, especially since today we were going to try taking Sierra on a long walk before her Dog Club time. Once we'd reached Market Street we split up to pick up our club dogs.

As soon as Gus heard me turn the key in the lock of his front door he bounded into the entryway, nails scratching lightly on the wooden floor as he waited for me.

"Who's a good doggy?" I asked him, coming in and closing the door behind me. Gus's mouth was slightly open in what looked just like a smile as he butted his head gently against me, eager to be petted.

I was happy to oblige. I scratched behind his ears, then gave his back a good rub. Gus panted happily.

"Are you ready to go play?" I asked him, reaching for the leash set out on the table.

He quivered with excitement as I snapped it on, then pranced beside me out of the house and down the street. A few minutes later we were at the dog park, where we met up with Coco, Popsicle, and Humphrey. And of course Kim and Taylor too. We took the dogs off their leashes and let them run together.

"I checked our Dog Club email last night and we got a message from a woman who's interested," I said, sitting on one of the benches on the edge of the park. There was one other owner there, an older woman whose little tan dog began playing chase with Popsicle and Coco.

"Oh, cool," Taylor said. "Did she sign up?"

"She's going to think about it," I said. "But Mrs. McDermott said she loves our blog." Kim grinned. "And she said the dog pictures are fabulous." Now Taylor was smiling too.

"What kind of dog does she have?" Kim asked.

"A mix. Mrs. McDermott said he's black and tan, with floppy ears. And he's really big."

Kim's smile faded. "I'm not sure we can handle another big dog," she said. "Not until we have Sierra behaving."

I hadn't thought of that but Kim was right. "Well, maybe he's big but very calm," I said.

"That would work," Kim said. "And we should get

going. I think we're a little late."

That was my fault—good thing I wasn't trying to prove my lack of flightiness to my friends!

We headed for the shelter. As we opened the door I expected to be bombarded by Sierra but instead we were met with happy barks and kisses from Boxer, Hattie, Lily, Daisy, and of course, Mr. Smashmouth, who raced over to me as fast as his little legs could carry him. As soon as I had Gus off his leash I picked up Mr. Smashmouth.

"Where's Sierra?" Taylor asked Tim.

"Caley took her out already," he said. "Mr. Finnegan dropped her off a little early and we figured it was better to get going before the club dogs got here."

"Good thinking," Kim said.

Alice came out of her office. Today she was wearing her Roxbury Park Dog Club T-shirt and so was Tim. "We all match," I said happily, since Kim and Taylor were wearing theirs too.

But then I realized we didn't match because I wasn't

wearing mine. "Yikes," I said, setting down Mr. Smashmouth and grabbing my backpack. I'd forgotten to put on my shelter clothes again!

I pawed through my stuff but after searching for a full minute, even taking everything out, I saw that it was worse than forgetting to put them on: I'd forgotten to bring them at all.

"I wish I had gym clothes or something to lend you," Taylor said sympathetically. She was throwing a ball for Boxer and Lily but had noticed my predicament.

"Thanks," I said with a sigh. This was definitely not going to show my mom that I was remembering things more. Though maybe I'd get lucky and could slip my school clothes in the washing machine before she got home. For now there was nothing to do but play with the dogs. So I did.

We took all the dogs out for a rowdy game of fetch, then Taylor and I took some of the smaller dogs—and the lazier ones like sweet Humphrey—back inside while Kim and Tim stayed out with the others.

Humphrey collapsed in the corner, clearly exhausted from the game. Hattie brought a tennis ball over to Taylor, who pitched it across the room. Hattie and Popsicle raced after it but Mr. Smashmouth stayed with me.

Alice came out of her office, pulling on a sweater. "Do you girls mind if I run a few errands?" she asked. "I'll be back before the club dog owners come for pickup."

"We're fine," I said. "Take your time."

"Thanks," she said, then headed out.

"Want to help me take a quiz?" I asked Mr. Smashmouth, settling on the floor and pulling him into my lap. "I'm trying to find the perfect pet and I bet you can help me." I slipped my phone out of my pocket and clicked on the quiz I'd found earlier. "Okay, first question: what is your favorite color?"

"How will that help you find a pet?" Taylor asked. "That sounds more like a quiz for redecorating your room."

"It says it figures out your personality and then

matches you with the perfect pet," I said.

Taylor shrugged. "Whatever works I guess." Hattie had picked up a pull toy and Taylor headed across the room to play with it, leaving me and Mr. Smashmouth to the quiz.

"My favorite color is aqua," I told Mr. Smashmouth, who tipped his head like he understood me. Kim was the one who could really talk to dogs but I felt like my bond with Mr. Smashmouth was special and we did understand each other. "But aqua isn't one of the options so I'll just go with blue." I clicked the answer and then waited for the next question.

Mr. Smashmouth snuggled even deeper into my lap and let out a contented sigh. I ran my hands along his soft ears. "You're a sweetie" I told him. "And here's the next question: What is your favorite flower? The choices are rose, tulip, carnation, or orchid. I like lilacs best, but what do you say we go with orchid? They're kind of exotic." Mr. Smashmouth seemed to agree so I clicked on orchid.

We spent the next few minutes finishing the quiz, with Taylor chiming in a few times.

"Okay, this is it," I said, after clicking for the final result. "My perfect pet is a . . ." I waited for it to appear. "A snake! Wait, a snake? Ew! That is *so* not my perfect pet." Taylor and I started laughing and I swear Mr. Smashmouth was laughing with us.

I bent down and buried my face in his soft tummy. Just then I heard the front door of the shelter open and Taylor say, "Hi, Mrs. Brown." It was my mom!

I scrambled to my feet and saw my mom staring at me. Well, more at Mr. Smashmouth, who was still snug in my arms. She was probably thinking about all the fur I was getting on my clothes. This was a nightmare!

"Hi, Mom," I said, setting Mr. Smashmouth on the ground and almost running over to her. "Is everything okay?" My mom had never come to the shelter before and I was realizing there might be a problem.

Then my mom held up the plastic bag with my shelter clothes. "I was home getting a file and I saw that you'd forgotten these," she said, passing me the bag. "I thought I'd bring them by so you wouldn't ruin your school clothes, but I guess I'm too late."

"They'll be fine after I wash them," I assured her. "They're not dirty at all."

My mom glanced at Mr. Smashmouth, who had trotted over to Humphrey and was playing with a ball. I wondered if I should try to get my mom to meet him. I mean, who wouldn't fall in love with his sweet little face? Plus Cavachons, Mr. Smashmouth's breed, didn't shed much, which I knew would impress her. But before I could say anything else my mom was already headed out, probably worried about getting fur on her crisp red suit. "I'll put the clothes in the wash as soon as I get home," I called after her.

She waved and then headed out. I slumped against the wall. That had not gone well at all. How was I going to prove I'd changed when I kept making the same old mistakes?

I heard a small yip and looked down. Mr.

Smashmouth was at my feet, his sweet face concerned. I scooped him up and cuddled him close, just as the sounds of one very rambunctious dog came from outside the front door.

"I think Caley and Sierra are back," I said to Taylor, whose eyes got big. She headed for the safety of Alice's office but it was too late: the door opened and in bounded Sierra, wild as ever.

Oscar flew from the room while Hattie and Popsicle took off for a far corner. Humphrey roused from his nap and took off after them. And Mr. Smashmouth burrowed deeper into my arms.

"How did it go?" I asked Caley.

"You know, it seemed like it was working toward the end," she said, running a hand through her short, windswept hair. "She was walking instead of running and the last few blocks she stopped straining against the leash."

"That seems good," I said.

"Yeah," Caley agreed. "But look at her now."

Sierra was running frantic laps around the room.

"It's like the walk never happened," Caley said with a sigh.

"I guess she's just excited to see the other dogs," I said.

As though to prove my point the back door opened and Boxer, Lily, Gus, and Coco came bouncing in, making Sierra go nuts. She galloped toward them at breakneck speed and Tim, who was coming in behind the dogs, jumped back.

"Whoa," he said as Coco, Gus, and Boxer raced after Sierra, turning the shelter into a dog tornado. Lily didn't run but she stood in the center of the room barking loudly, so that didn't help.

Tim called out something that was impossible to hear over the noise, but then he ushered Sierra toward the backyard, so clearly he was telling us his plan. He shut the door before any of the other dogs could get out.

"Yikes," Kim said. I hadn't even noticed her come in. "I guess the walk didn't help."

"Actually Caley said she did calm down at the end," I said. "But I think seeing the other dogs revved her back up."

"It doesn't take much to rev that dog," Caley said. She was looking out the window into the yard, where Sierra was trying to dig her hole again.

Kim, Taylor, and I exchanged a look.

"I guess it's back to the drawing board," Kim said.

So it was. I was still sure we'd come up with something. But even I had to admit things couldn't go on like they were.

We were running out of time and options.

9

"Um, you guys, is it supposed to look like this?" Taylor asked, sounding worried. She was standing in front of the stove at my house, stirring a big saucepan of what we hoped would turn out to be Turkish delight. But so far it wasn't going that well.

"I think we made a mistake trying to double the recipe the first time we tried it," I said. That had been Kim's idea, since we'd have to double it when we made it for the festival, to be sure we had enough for everyone.

"But why bother with a smaller amount?" Kim said, coming over to the stove. "Then it's like we're doing it a totally new way when we double the recipe for the whole grade." That was exactly what she had said before.

"More can go wrong when you work with bigger amounts," Taylor said. "Like, I don't think this is supposed to look like tiny rocks, but it does."

I'd been cleaning up the sugar we'd spilled on the counter but I came to look over Taylor's other shoulder.

"I don't think that's right," I said, staring into the pan, which contained boiling sugar and water. I looked at the recipe next to the stove. "It's supposed to just be liquid."

"I probably didn't stir it enough," Taylor fretted.

"Don't worry, we can just stir it a lot now," Kim said, grabbing a wooden spoon and dipping it into the hot liquid. She whipped the spoon around the pot and a spray of sugar water flew out and onto the stove. Something else we'd need to clean before my mom got home. Which was a lot sooner than I would have liked. Somehow this whole venture, which was supposed to be ninety minutes, was taking over the whole afternoon.

"Gently," Taylor told Kim, who slowed her spoon. "I think it's getting better," she said after a minute.

I peeked in and sure enough the pebbles were gone and it looked like liquid. I sighed with relief. There was still a lot to clean but at least the candy was on the right track.

"Okay, now we put this aside and boil the other ingredients," Taylor said. "I'll get the water and cornstarch.

"I'll get the cream of tartar," I said, looking at the recipe.

We poured everything into a new saucepan and Kim turned on the burner.

"Here's the rosewater," Taylor said. We'd ordered it special off the internet and it had come in a pretty little glass bottle.

"Wait, I think we add that later," I said.

But it was too late, Taylor had already put it in.

"Uh-oh," she said.

"I'm sure it's not a big deal," I said, noting the tightness in her face. But secretly I wasn't so sure. I knew it mattered that the ingredients go in when they were supposed to. Plus I was feeling anxious about how the kitchen was covered in spills, so I wasn't in the best place to be reassuring.

"It's just a practice run anyway," Taylor said, trying to calm everyone down. "We're working out the kinks so it'll be perfect when we make it for the festival."

"Right," Kim said, taking a deep breath. "Okay, Taylor, do you want to stir it while I help Sash clean up a bit?"

That sounded great. Kim and I made quick work of the sugar on the counter, the crusted sugar water on the stove, and the light dusting of cornstarch on the floor.

Now I was feeling a lot better. "What's next?" I asked.

"I think this is done," Taylor said, looking at the pot she'd been stirring. "It's supposed to have the consistency of glue." She lifted a spoon and the sticky, gloppy mixture clung to it, then slid off slowly in a slithering mass.

I couldn't help wrinkling my nose. "It doesn't look so good."

"It smells good though," Kim pointed out. "That rose is sweet."

"Should we add more rosewater?" I asked. "Since we're supposed to put it in now?"

Kim frowned. "I'm not sure," she said. "We don't want it to taste too flowery."

"Sash, can you get the other pot?" Taylor asked. "We need to combine them and then let it all simmer together. Then we can figure out the rosewater."

"I have to go in a few minutes," Kim said, looking at the clock on the stove.

"Me too," Taylor said. "But Sash, I think it's pretty easy to finish up, just some stirring and then pouring it into the baking pan and letting it cool overnight." We'd already gotten the pan greased and ready.

"I can handle that," I said, bringing the other pot over to Taylor.

"We'll help you clean before we go," Kim said. "Though there's not much left to do."

It did look good. My mom was definitely going to be impressed.

I lifted the pot full of syrupy mixture to pour it into the saucepan that had the boiling sugar water and lemon but the moment it hit the water, some drops flew up and hit the inside of my wrist. I jerked back instinctively and both pots clattered to the floor, splashing hot sugar water and the sticky cornstarch mix across the kitchen.

The three of us gasped.

"Oh no!" Taylor exclaimed, looking panicked as she gazed around at the once-spotless kitchen that was now coated with slime.

"I can't believe this," Kim said.

I was speechless, staring in horror at the incredible mess surrounding us.

Taylor was the first to recover. "Okay, let's start cleaning up. Sash, where do you guys keep rags and sponges?"

"I think we'll need a mop too," Kim said.

I tried to take a deep breath and calm down so I could take charge but my chest was too tight. This was a disaster. It would take ages to clean and I couldn't let Taylor and Kim get in trouble for getting home late.

Kim was searching in the pantry for supplies and Taylor was rummaging under the sink. The sight of my two friends trying to fix things pushed me to get it together.

"You guys, I can take care of it," I said. "It's late."

"We can't leave you with so much work," Kim said. But I could see her forehead creased with worry at the thought of being late. Not to mention the fact that our project was a total fiasco and I knew how stressed she was about our grade.

"Really, it's okay," I said. "I have a while before my mom gets home. I can get it done. And you guys need to get going."

Taylor and Kim exchanged a look.

"If you're sure, I really should get home and start dinner," Taylor said. "Anna has to stay late at school for a young engineers meeting and she asked me to get things ready."

We all knew what would happen if Taylor messed that up. Anna wasn't exactly understanding.

"Go, I'm fine, really," I said, trying to sound upbeat as I shooed them out. I did have at least an hour before my mom got home. That should be enough time to wipe up the layer of gunk covering everything. Maybe.

Though when I got back to the kitchen after walking them out and saw goop coating the counter, puddles of it all over the floor, and spots of it on the fronts of all the appliances I kind of wanted to cry. But that wouldn't help, so I grabbed one of the sponges Taylor had gotten out and got to work.

I was making pretty good progress when I heard a sound that made my heart stop: my mother's key in the front door. She was home early! I scrubbed desperately at the floor but I knew it was no use. There was at least an hour's worth of cleanup yet to do.

I heard my mom slip off her shoes and then walk down the hall, her steps coming closer. My heart started thumping hard in my chest as she came nearer and nearer. This was not going to be good.

Sure enough, when she reached the doorway her hands flew to her chest, as though the sight of the filthy kitchen might give her a heart attack. Her eyes were wide like a zombie was walking toward her and her mouth fell open. Yeah, this was bad, all right.

"Mom, it's going to be okay," I said, standing up. I realized I had some of the gunk on my face but when I tried to wipe it off I just glopped even more on.

"What—what happened?" my mom stuttered.

"Taylor, Kim, and I had a little accident when we

were trying to cook our project for social studies," I said.

My mom gazed around the room, which practically glistened from its slimy coating. "You call this a *little* accident?" she asked.

"No one was hurt," I said, hoping that information would help. And I realized we were lucky none of us had been hit by the hot liquid when it flew all over the place.

"Well, I'm glad to hear that," my mom said. Her shock was subsiding and now she just looked disappointed in me, which was the worst. "I'll change and then we can clean this up. I don't think we'll have time to cook so we can just order pizza or something."

I hated how beaten-down she sounded. She worked hard all day and now she was coming home to more work—work made by me and the fact that I hadn't been careful enough. Again.

"Mom, I'm sorry," I said.

"Accidents happen," she said. "But maybe next time

you could be more careful."

"We will," I said. My shoulders sagged as I watched her walk out of the room. My plan had totally backfired. Instead of showing my mom how I'd changed, it showed her I was just as flighty as ever.

There was definitely no asking for a pet now.

10

The next day the weather matched my mood: dreary, gray, and by the time school let out, rainy. We each ran to pick up our club dogs and then met up at the shelter instead of our usual stop at the park. Once we were all inside the dogs were extra energetic, running around and barking away.

"Hey, girls," Caley called. She and Alice were heading into the food area and the dogs all ran to see if maybe dinner was early today.

"Sorry, guys," Alice said with a laugh. "We're just checking how much food to order." She turned to us with a smile. "We'll be done in a sec."

The front door opened and Tim came in, shaking rain off his black raincoat. "It's really coming down out there," he said. "And is it me or does this place reek of wet dog fur?"

It definitely did. I went to change into my shelter clothes and when I came out Kim and Taylor were throwing tennis balls for Coco, Lily, Gus, and Popsicle. Alice was back in her office. Tim was on the floor playing tug-of-war with Humphrey while Caley was tossing Boxer's favorite Frisbee to him, Daisy, and Hattie. And where was Mr. Smashmouth? Right at my feet, waiting to be picked up. I happily obliged.

"Hello, little guy," I said, giving him a kiss. Then I headed over to Taylor and Kim so that he could play fetch with the others.

"Was your mom really upset about the kitchen?"

Kim asked. She'd had to retake a math test over lunch, so we hadn't had time to catch up yet.

"No, it was worse," I said. "She was disappointed."

"Ugh, I hate that," Kim said sympathetically. Gus dropped a ball at her feet and she patted his head before sending it across the room for him. "Did it take a long time to clean?"

"It wasn't bad," I said. I was pretty much lying. It had taken my mom and me almost two hours to scrub up all the gunk and wipe everything down so it wasn't sticky anymore. The kitchen still stank of rose, which was now the smell I most hated. And my mom had been too tired to even eat the pizza once it arrived. But there was no point in telling Kim and Taylor about that. It wasn't their fault they'd had to leave.

"It sounds like a rough night though," Kim said.

I guess I still looked pretty down.

"I have something to cheer you up," Taylor said, pulling some paper out of her pocket. "It's a pet quiz

I downloaded last night. It's got fifty questions and it's guaranteed to find the perfect pet for anyone and everyone."

"Sounds good," I said, my interest piqued despite yesterday's setback. There was still plenty of time to show my mom how responsible I was. And with this foolproof quiz I'd be ready with the ideal family pet when she said yes! "Thanks."

There was barking outside the shelter and then the sound of scratching on the front door. The dogs in the shelter seemed to freeze and Taylor began inching toward the safety of Alice's office. Sierra had arrived.

Tim opened the door for Mr. Finnegan while Kim went to help stop Sierra before she could take off with her leash still attached. Sierra's nails ground into the floor as she strained against both Kim and Mr. Finnegan, but Kim managed to get the leash off before setting her free.

The little dogs had already fled, so Sierra had a clear path as she took off around the shelter.

"I'll see you later," Mr. Finnegan said. "Thank you."

"Let's get these dogs playing," Tim said, rubbing his hands together. Then he grabbed a green ball and threw it high in the air. When it bounced back down Coco, Lily, Gus, and Sierra took off after it.

"Want to see if we can get the little dogs to come out?" Kim asked me, Caley, and Taylor.

"Definitely," I said, and Taylor and Caley nodded.

We picked up some tennis balls and chew toys and headed to the other side of the shelter, near the cages. Then we began coaxing the little dogs out, being sure to keep their toys far from Sierra.

Mr. Smashmouth came over to me right away and Popsicle and Daisy went to Kim. Hattie stayed in her cage, so Taylor went over and began petting her in there. Humphrey had settled in for a nap in the far corner. Caley pet him for a moment, then picked up Boxer's Frisbee. "He's not little but I think he needs some one-on-one attention," she said. Boxer pranced at her feet, clearly agreeing.

And for a few minutes everything was great. The dogs played happily, the humans were having fun, and everyone seemed relaxed.

But then Caley tossed Boxer's Frisbee close to Sierra, who lunged for it. Boxer ran over, ready to play, but Sierra ran away with it. And when Boxer followed, close at her heels, she dropped the Frisbee and nipped at him.

"Sierra!" Caley called, rushing over.

Sierra ignored her and snapped at Boxer again. This time Boxer flattened his ears and growled.

"Boxer, come," Caley called, now sounding slightly panicked.

But Boxer was locked in a battle for his beloved Frisbee and he growled again, this time louder.

Alice was out of her office like a shot. "Boxer, come," she said in her gentle but no-nonsense way. And this time Boxer came. "Kim, can you take him to his cage to calm him?" she asked. "And Tim, will you please take Sierra out to the back porch for a few minutes?"

They both did as she asked and order was restored. But my heart was still pounding crazily in my chest and I could see that both Caley and Kim were pale, while Taylor looked close to a panic attack. That had been bad and we were lucky it wasn't worse. What if we'd had a real dog fight on our hands?

"How's he doing?" Alice asked Kim, who was walking back to the center of the room with Boxer.

"He's fine," Kim said. "But maybe we should put away his Frisbee for the rest of the day. I don't think he's going to want to share it."

"Good idea," Alice said. "Though I think our problems may go deeper than that."

"We haven't figured out how to settle Sierra into the club," Kim agreed. She began throwing a red rubber ball for Boxer, Lily, and Coco.

"We've been trying," Caley said. She still looked a bit shaken up but was on the floor petting Hattie and Popsicle.

"And I know we'll figure it out," I added.

But Alice frowned. "I'm not so sure about that," she said. "The other dogs are scared of Sierra and one of them could have gotten hurt today."

I hated that she was right but there was no denying it.

"I know you girls want to help," she went on. "But it's possible that the Dog Club may not be right for every dog. Perhaps Sierra isn't a good fit for what we do here."

Kim, Taylor, and I exchanged a stricken look. We couldn't kick Sierra out of the Dog Club! If we did, no Roxbury Park dog owner would ever sign up for the club again. We needed our word of mouth to be positive, letting potential customers know that the Roxbury Park Dog Club was the perfect place for their dogs. Not a place where some dogs fit in and others were asked to leave.

"Alice, let us keep trying," I begged. "I know we can find a way to make it work."

Alice bit her lip for a moment, clearly considering my request. "What ideas do you have?" she finally asked.

I let out the breath I'd been holding. She was giving us another chance! But I knew it was probably the last one, so we had to make it count.

"Taking her on a long walk seemed to help," Caley said, "at least at first."

"It was coming back here and seeing the other dogs that got her worked up," Kim said.

"Oh, I've got it!" I almost shouted. "We take Sierra on a group walk before coming to the shelter. That way she gets exercise and exposure to the other dogs so it's not as overwhelming when she arrives." I was so excited about my idea that I almost jumped up and down.

Alice nodded slowly. "It's worth a try, I suppose," she said. "As long as you can convince Mr. Finnegan to let you pick Sierra up for the club."

"I can, I know I can," I bubbled. I was already composing my speech in my head.

And by the time he came to pick up Sierra I was ready. I'd practiced my pitch with Taylor, Kim, and Caley, and Tim had promised to keep Sierra busy while

I spoke to her owner. Gus, Daisy, and Coco had been picked up by the time Mr. Finnegan arrived, which helped too—less dogs to rile Sierra up.

"How did everything go today?" Mr. Finnegan asked after greeting an exuberant Sierra.

"Well, she was a bit wound up," I began. Caley had come up with that phrase and we all agreed it was very diplomatic. "And I had an idea that might help."

"I'd love to hear it," Mr. Finnegan said. His eyes were on Sierra, now playing a ferocious game of tug-of-war with Tim, who was looking tired. Hopefully Mr. Finnegan wouldn't notice that part.

"It seems like when Sierra arrives at the shelter she's got a lot of energy," I began. "And she's very excited to see the other dogs."

"That's certainly true," Mr. Finnegan agreed.

"So we were thinking you could use the Roxbury Park Dog Club pickup service," I said. "One of us would come to your house to get Sierra for the club. We'd have at least one other dog and we'd take them both on a walk before bringing them here, to get out some of that energy and to let Sierra begin socializing with other dogs before arriving at the shelter."

Mr. Finnegan rubbed his chin for a moment. "I'm not sure," he said slowly. "She's a lot to handle, even on her own."

"We've taken her out for walks before without any problem," Caley said.

"And it seemed to calm her down a bit," I added.

"But are you sure one of you could manage her plus another dog?" he asked, sounding doubtful. "That seems like a lot to me."

"Yes, absolutely," I said, trying to sound relaxed even though sweat was pricking my temples. We needed him to agree to this and I knew that meant presenting him with a rational and calm argument. "All of us here have a lot of experience working with multiple dogs."

"That's true," he said thoughtfully.

"We'd take Sierra with one of the less playful dogs,"

Kim said. "And that would probably have a soothing effect on her."

"Perhaps it would," Mr. Finnegan said. It seemed like he was almost convinced, so I took a deep breath and gave it everything I had. "I really think this is the perfect way for Sierra to transition into the club time." That was another Caley phrase. "She'll be able to adjust to time out of the house and time with other dogs in smaller steps. So when she gets here it won't be overwhelming. She'll be more prepared and everything will go better from there."

I was worried the last part didn't sound quite as polished but Taylor gave me a thumbs-up behind Mr. Finnegan's back, so it couldn't have been too bad.

There was a pause as Mr. Finnegan considered, then nodded. "Okay, let's give it a try," he said as Sierra bounded over and jumped up on his shoulders.

I suppressed my squeal of delight until they'd both left.

"Great job," Kim cheered.

"Yeah, you sold it to them like a pro," Caley said.

Taylor gave me another thumbs-up and even Alice was smiling.

Only Tim looked worried. "Now we just have to hope it works," he said.

11

"Hi, hon, how was dance?" my mom asked when I climbed into the car after class, leaning over to give me a kiss. She sounded cheerful and I knew that the slimed kitchen incident was now fully behind us. In general my mom didn't hold on to grudges for long, thank goodness. Because I'd taken that quiz Taylor had given me and had the perfect pet ready to pitch to her! Plus I'd come up with an idea to show her how serious I'd be about caring for a pet. But first I had a few examples of how responsible I was that I needed to tell her about, to set the stage just right.

"Dance was great," I said, sitting back in my seat as she eased the car out of the parking lot and onto Olive Avenue. "And guess what? Madame Florence chose me to manage the dressing room during our winter show!"

It actually sounded like a bigger deal than it was: the manager was just the one who was in charge of going to the real stage manager if there was any kind of costume problem. And all of us had some kind of job for the show. But still, mine sounded good and I could tell from the pride on my mom's face that she was pleased.

"Congratulations," she said warmly. "Madame Florence must think you're very capable if she chose you for that job."

Madame Florence did think I was capable—or more like she expected it of all of us and so we were. But I was glad that my mom was happy about the job. And I knew she'd like my news about Sierra too. I'd been saving it for the right moment and clearly this was it.

"Guess what else?" I said. "I came up with a plan to help integrate Sierra into the Dog Club, to make her transition from home to the shelter go more smoothly."

I could tell by my mom's grin that she liked the Caley words as much as Mr. Finnegan had. "Good for you," she said. "Tell me about it."

"She needs some exercise first thing, so I'm going to pick her up and take her for a walk before going to the shelter," I said. "And she gets really worked up seeing the other dogs, so I'm going to bring Gus along on the walk, to kind of ease her into things."

My mom was nodding. "That is a good idea. And her owner agreed?"

"Yes, I told him about it and he thought it could work," I said, feeling a glow as I remembered how Mr. Finnegan had finally agreed to our plan. "Alice said we should give it a try too. So I'll be getting Gus and Sierra and walking them before our next Dog Club."

"Wonderful," my mom said. "Good for you for coming up with a smart plan." Instead of turning onto our street she kept going straight. "I have to pick up a few things at the grocery," she said.

That was even more than I could have hoped for: we would be right by Paula's Pet Emporium. It was like a sign that now was the time to finally convince my mom about a pet. So I took a deep breath and dove in. "I took a quiz Taylor gave me, about the best pet for our family," I said, looking out the window instead of at my mom. I didn't want to see her reaction until I'd said everything. "And it said a chinchilla would be the best fit for us. I looked them up online last night and it seems like it could really work. They're neat and quiet and the article said they're affectionate too."

We were stopped at a light and I snuck a quick peek at my mom. Her expression was neutral, which was way better than negative, so I went on.

"I know you're worried I'll forget to take care of it so I came up with an idea," I said. "I'll make a weekly chart of her feeding schedule and I'll put it up on the fridge. Every day after I feed her I'll check it off, so you'll know it's done and so I won't forget." I crossed my fingers and braced myself. "What do you think?"

"Her?" my mom said, turning the car into the lot in front of Old Farm Market. "So you want a girl?"

"Yeah, because I was thinking we could call her Pippi," I said.

My mom reached over and patted my hand. "I used to love reading you those books," she said softly.

"Yeah, they were the best," I said. I spoke softly too, not wanting to break the spell. This was the very first time that her response wasn't an immediate no, and I didn't want to do anything to mess that up.

We went into the market, where I helped with the shopping, making sure to get the exact right milk and yogurt, and not asking for any cookies or treats. When we were in line to pay I put everything on the conveyer belt, then turned to my mom.

"Is it okay if I go to the pet store?" I asked. "I know

they have chinchillas and I want to just take a quick look."

"Sure, honey," my mom said. She was a bit distracted but her response still seemed pretty positive.

I practically skipped over to the pet store.

"How can I help you?" Today it was a man behind the counter, who looked sleepy, like he'd just woken up from a nap.

"I want to see the chinchillas please," I said. It's possible I was a little loud because he winced a bit. But then he got a key from under the counter and led me over to a glass cage with four gray and white young chinchillas inside.

They were smaller than I'd thought, almost the size of mice. Actually they looked a lot like mice, though with bigger ears. Some of my excitement drained away as I watched them just sitting in a pile together, all mousy and not really doing anything.

"Want to hold one?" the man asked.

"Go ahead, hon," my mom said.

I hadn't seen her walk up and her reaction nearly made me fall over in shock. Even more amazing was the way she was looking at the chinchillas and actually smiling.

The man reached into the case and pulled out a chinchilla, handing it gently to me. It fit in one hand and its little claws dug into the soft skin of my palm. I tried to move it around but the claws still scratched.

"They're very soft," the man said.

My mom reached out a finger and stroked its side. "Oh, it really is," she said.

I pet it gently on the other side. It was soft. But it just sat there in my hand looking bored. And mousy. Not that there was anything wrong with mice but a mouse wasn't exactly my dream pet. Especially one that just sat there doing nothing.

"Let me give you our pamphlet on chinchillas," the man said, walking to the front of the store and grabbing one from the wire display by the register. When he came back I handed him the chinchilla and he gave me the pamphlet.

"We're open tomorrow at ten if you want to come back for this little guy," he said.

"Actually I think we'd need a girl," my mom said, giving me a wink.

As we walked out I knew I should feel over the moon at my mom's reaction. But somehow I didn't, I just felt flat.

"They're cute," my mom said, smiling at me.

It was hard to smile back.

"Maybe we should think about getting one," she said as we drove home. She glanced over at me, almost quizzical, as though to gauge my reaction.

"Okay, yeah, let's think about it," I said, working to sound enthusiastic. What was wrong with me? Getting a pet had been my dream forever and after all the careful arguments she'd shot down, this one was finally looking like a yes. I should be jumping up and down! Well, we were in the car so I couldn't actually jump but I should at least be bouncing a little. But I wasn't. I felt more like a soda that had lost all its fizz. Maybe I was just hungry?

Even after a dinner of Old Farm Market's tasty minestrone soup and just-baked bread, I was still feeling hollow inside. I helped my mom clean up after dinner and then went upstairs, where I pulled out the brochure on chinchillas. If I learned more about them maybe they would seem more exciting.

The good news was that it turned out chinchillas were playful. But the bad news was that they were crepuscular, which meant that they were most active at dawn and dusk, two times I was pretty busy. Plus they mostly played with their toys in their cage, which wasn't that exciting. No fetch or tug-of-war. Reading about them made me feel even flatter, if that was possible.

So later that night, when I went down for a snack during my study break, I took the brochure in to my mom's study.

"Mom, I don't think a chinchilla will work for us," I said, showing her one of the pages. "It says here that you need to give them a bath in ashes once a week, to keep their fur clean."

I thought she'd be surprised but instead she nodded knowingly, almost like she had expected me to say something like this. Maybe she'd picked up on my lack of enthusiasm in the car. "That doesn't seem so good," she said. "It could get pretty messy."

"Yeah," I agreed. "Sorry I didn't notice it before."

My mom smiled at me. "I'm glad you caught it now," she said.

I headed back upstairs, still not sure why I didn't want the one pet my mom had finally agreed to. I remembered all the books my mom gave me about puberty and growing up. Had I somehow outgrown wanting a pet and not even realized it? But when I thought about how much I loved my time with the dogs at the shelter, especially Mr. Smashmouth, I knew that wasn't it.

All I could conclude was that the quiz was wrong and a chinchilla just wasn't the right pet. So over the weekend I decided I'd take some more quizzes and do more research—now that my mom was finally starting to consider a pet, I needed to be ready!

12

"Are you ready for Sierra?" Kim asked when I arrived at her locker after the final bell had rung.

"Totally," I said. I'd been thinking about it for days. My plan was to get Gus first, since I didn't want to risk letting Sierra loose in Gus's house. He and I would go get Sierra, bring her to the dog park to play a bit with the other club dogs, and then take a walk together before heading over to the shelter. And by the time we got there, Sierra would have gotten out her wild energy and be ready to play nicely with the other dogs. Or at least not terrify them.

"Hey," Taylor said, coming up from behind me. She was twisting a braid tightly around her fingers.

"What's wrong?" I asked.

"Nothing really," Taylor said, but her face was tense. "I just messed up in science and kind of got in trouble."

"What happened?" Kim asked, immediately concerned.

"Brianna accidently gave me the wrong size beaker when she was passing them out to everyone," Taylor said. "And my experiment went all over my lab table."

"That sucks," Kim said, squeezing Taylor's arm. Kim totally understood school problems.

But I was more worried about Brianna problems. "Did Brianna give anyone else the wrong size?" I asked, shifting my backpack from one shoulder to the other.

"No, but it was an honest mistake," Taylor said. "I mean, she just passed them out randomly from the box Ms. Lewis gave her."

I wasn't so sure. "I don't think I trust Brianna," I said as Kim closed her locker and we joined the crowd heading out of school. "I don't like how she calls you 'new girl.'"

Taylor laughed. "I don't mind," she said. "I *am* the new girl. But thanks for having my back just in case."

"Always," I said. If it didn't bother Taylor I was willing to let it go, at least for now.

"Do you guys want to sleep over on Saturday?" Taylor asked as we walked outside and ducked past a group of kids throwing a football. "We can do another trial run of Turkish delight and finish up the poster."

"Sounds great," I said. It would be fun to make the Turkish delight as long as we weren't at my house.

I looked at Kim, waiting for her to agree, but she was biting her lip. "I'm not sure," she said slowly. "I have a big math test on Monday and I should probably study."

"We can help you study for it after we make the Turkish delight," I said.

"And we can ask Anna for strategies," Taylor added. "She might be a pain but she's a pain who's really good at math."

"Okay," Kim agreed. "As long as we make sure there's enough time for it."

"We will," I promised.

"And it will be good to get our social studies project done," Taylor added.

"Don't forget we'll need stuff for milk shakes too," I reminded her. Our sleepover tradition was to make amazing milk shakes with add-ins like M&M's, peanut butter, and my favorite, rainbow sprinkles.

"Good thinking," Taylor said. "I'll make sure we have supplies."

We'd reached the street and I was eager to get Sierra. "I'll see you guys at the park," I said, heading off for Gus's house.

I jogged most of the way and it just took a few minutes to get Gus leashed up and out the door. "We're going to get your friend Sierra," I told him. Gus hadn't exactly played with her before but he wasn't one of the dogs that hid from her either. I was confident that the two of them together would have fun.

The Finnegans lived just two blocks from Main Street, in a small white house with green shutters and lilac bushes lining the front walk. It was hard to imagine living in a little house with such a big dog! Though they did have a good-sized backyard that I noticed had a high fence. I hoped it went down deep too, so Sierra couldn't dig her way out like she wanted to at Dog Club.

Sierra began barking as soon as she heard us walk up the front steps.

"Hey, Sierra," I said as I opened the door. Sierra leaped up on my shoulders and I staggered backward. Gus barked in alarm. But I righted myself quickly and we walked inside.

Sierra was racing around her house in excitement. It was kind of cute but a little worrisome—what if I couldn't get her leash on? Gus sat beside me watching Sierra but luckily not trying to join her.

"Sierra, come," I called.

Nothing.

"Sierra, come," I said as firmly as I could.

Sierra flew through the entryway and into the living room. This was not going well. But then I saw the sticky note left next to Sierra's leash on the dresser by the door. *Dog treats inside top drawer to help Sierra stay still for her leash.* Perfect!

I located the treats, then shook the bag. Sierra came racing in and leaped up on me, but this time I was ready. I snapped her leash onto her collar and then pulled her down. "Sit," I said firmly.

Sierra wagged her tail.

"Sit," I said again, holding up the bag.

Sierra sat. "Good girl," I told her, giving her a treat, which she wolfed down. I gave one to Gus too since he'd been waiting so nicely. Then the three of us headed out into the sunny afternoon.

I knew to have a tight hold on Sierra's leash, and good thing because we'd walked about thirty seconds before she spotted a squirrel and tried to chase it. She nearly pulled my shoulder out of the socket but I kept my fingers wrapped tight around the handle and Sierra's ears drooped as the squirrel made its getaway.

"You can run at the park," I told her.

Halfway down Main Street I switched arms since the one holding Sierra was getting tired. Gus was being his usual sweet self, if a bit more subdued, but he didn't seem scared or upset by Sierra. So far my plan was working.

Kim, Humphrey, Popsicle, Taylor, and Coco had arrived at the park before us and as soon as Sierra saw them she lunged forward. "Hold on," I told her, bracing myself so I wouldn't fall over.

"She's giving you a workout," Kim observed, sounding slightly concerned.

"It's fine, I have dancer muscles," I reassured her. Though I had to admit I was looking forward to a little break at the park—Sierra was strong!

We were at the gate and Coco ran over to greet us.

That set Sierra off—she jumped up to put her paws on the top of the gate and her head whacked into my elbow. I jerked my arm back and somehow in that moment, the leash fell out of my hands. Sierra was off like a shot, bounding down the sidewalk, the leash trailing behind her.

In a panic I passed Gus to Kim and took off after Sierra. But the big dog had a good lead on me. I saw her turn on Elm Street but by the time I reached the corner, Sierra was gone.

My whole body was shaking as I walked back to the dog park.

"Where did she go?" Taylor asked, her eyes wide.

"I have no idea," I said, the words high and squeaky. "She just disappeared." Gus came and rubbed against my legs, clearly sensing my distress.

"We should go look for her," Taylor said.

"Yeah, but I have no idea where she went," I said. Despite the warmth of the day I felt all shivery. "You guys, this is really bad."

There was a terrible moment of silence. Then Kim cleared her throat. "It's going to be okay," she said, though her voice didn't sound right and her face was pale. "We need to get these guys to the shelter and then we'll see about finding Sierra."

"Should one of us maybe stay out and look for Sierra?" I asked. The longer we waited, the farther away she could be.

But Kim shook her head. "We have to get these guys safe and we have to tell Alice and the Finnegans what happened," she said, walking over to Humphrey and snapping on his leash. "We're going to need their help."

The thought of telling Alice and the Finnegans made me want to fall onto the ground and cry. But there wasn't time for that, not when we needed to find Sierra. So I took a shaking breath and began to help Taylor and Kim walk the dogs back to the shelter.

"Mr. Finnegan is on his way," Alice said, coming out of her office, her face drawn.

"I'm so sorry, Alice," I said, tears springing to my eyes. This was horrible for her and the shelter and the club—it was like in that split second I let Sierra get away, I'd ruined everything.

"Let's just focus on finding Sierra," Alice said, putting her hand on my shoulder for a moment. The warmth of it helped me choke back my tears. "I'll stay here to look after the dogs. The rest of you can search."

"We should split into pairs," Caley said. I'd never seen her look so serious, her normally rosy cheeks pale and her smile gone. "And each pair can check out a different part of town. Sierra has to be somewhere."

"Sounds good," Kim said. She and Taylor had stuck close to me ever since it happened. "Sasha and I can go west, back toward the dog park."

Just then the front door opened and Mr. Finnegan burst in. "Have you found her?" he asked. He was out of breath—clearly he had run all the way here.

"Mr. Finnegan," I began, but Alice held up a hand and I stopped.

"We haven't found her yet," Alice said in a soothing voice. "Our plan is to break into pairs and look for her. You and Tim can walk down Elm Street. That's where the girls last saw her."

I held my breath, waiting for Mr. Finnegan to start yelling about how irresponsible we were for letting Sierra go, but he just ran his hands through his hair, which was messy from his run, and said, "Let's go."

As we all filed for the door Alice beckoned me over. "Don't worry about apologizing right now," she told me quietly. "There will be time for that later, but now we need to focus all our energy on finding Sierra."

"Okay," I said. I really wanted to tell Mr. Finnegan how terrible I felt but I knew Alice was right: all that mattered right now was finding Sierra.

"Does everyone have their phones?" Tim asked when we were outside the shelter.

Everyone except for me nodded. Of course I'd forgotten mine like I forgot everything.

"As soon as you find her, text Alice and then the rest of us," Tim said.

And then we all fanned out, everyone moving as fast as they could.

Kim and I speed-walked down Main Street and now that it was just the two of us I could finally say everything I was thinking. "What if we don't find her and it gets too dark to search?" I said. "Or she gets hurt? Or someone dognaps her?"

Kim put an arm around my shoulders and hugged me. "None of that is going to happen," she said. "We're going to find her." She had made her voice confident but I saw the wrinkle of worry etched between her brows. She was concerned, and why wouldn't she be? Any of those things could happen, or worse, and we both knew it.

"It's all my fault," I said, my voice breaking.

"Sash, it was an accident," Kim said firmly. "Don't fall apart now. We need you to help look for Sierra."

She was right. I pushed my worries down and the

two of us ran toward the dog park. As we got close I saw that there were a few dogs playing together and for a moment I thought one toward the back corner might be Sierra. But then the dog bounded forward and it was a big collie, not our wild German shepherd.

"Let's go down Calico Drive," Kim said. She led the way, with me close on her heels. Every minute or so one of us called her name as we peered down driveways and behind trees, but there was no sign of Sierra. The sun was getting lower in the sky and I felt a chill creep over me, though I wasn't sure if it was the cold or knowing what I had done.

"I wonder if we should turn around," Kim said. Her face was in shadow but I could hear the anxiety in her voice.

Then her phone beeped with a text. Kim reached into her pocket so fast she fumbled the phone and nearly dropped it. But when she read the text a big smile came over her face. "Caley and Taylor found Sierra!" she said, throwing her arms around me. I hugged her back, hard, relief making my legs so weak I wasn't sure if I could stand on my own.

"Let's go back," Kim said after a minute.

I nodded, steadied myself, and we headed back to the shelter.

When we walked in the door everyone was smiling, the dogs were running around, and Sierra stood next to Mr. Finnegan, who held her leash tightly in one hand. He was talking to Alice and I rushed right over to them.

"It was my fault we lost Sierra," I told him. "And I'm so sorry." I didn't want him to think for one minute that Alice or any of the others were responsible for this.

"The last time she got loose it was my fault," Mr. Finnegan said, looking at me kindly. "And then it took us hours to track her down. So believe me, I understand how easily it can happen."

It was nice of him to say but I knew it had been my job to keep Sierra safe, and I'd totally let him and Alice and everyone down.

"Where did you guys find her?" Kim asked. She was petting Sierra, who looked slightly disappointed all the excitement had ended. She'd probably had fun frolicking around town on her own.

"In the Cotswalds' front yard chasing a squirrel," Caley said, coming up and putting an arm around my shoulders.

"That sounds like Sierra," Mr. Finnegan said affectionately. "Thank you so much for finding her."

"We're happy she's back safe and sound," Alice said. She spoke in a calm voice but I could see from the way that her ponytail was falling apart and the tightness in her face that she had been worried. Really worried. And she was probably still thinking about how bad this could have been and how lucky we were that Caley and Taylor had found Sierra so fast. I was certainly still thinking about it.

"I should get this girl home," Mr. Finnegan said, pulling a reluctant Sierra toward the exit. "Thank you again." The door closed softly behind them.

"Well, that was an afternoon of drama," Caley said, dragging her arm across her forehead in an exaggerated gesture of relief.

"Makes drama club look like naptime," Tim added with a grin.

Boxer came up to Caley, dropped his Frisbee at her feet, and wagged his tail hopefully. Caley obliged by throwing it across the room and Boxer, Coco, Gus, and Lily took off after it. Daisy brought a tug toy over to Taylor, who settled into the game, and Kim picked up a tennis ball for Popsicle. The phone rang and Alice went to her office to get it. Everyone was going back to the usual routine, everyone but me. I couldn't shake the cold feeling that had seeped into me when Sierra was lost, and the horrible knowledge that it was all my fault.

Something warm pressed against my leg and I looked down. Mr. Smashmouth was looking up at me, his expression concerned. I picked him up and hugged him close. He licked my cheek comfortingly, then wriggled in under my chin.

It didn't make me feel totally better; nothing could. But it sure did help.

13

"What's wrong, Sash?" my mom asked at dinner later that night. I was just pushing my food around my plate, unable to eat much, and of course she had noticed.

I didn't want to admit what had happened at the shelter but it felt too big to keep secret from her. "Remember how I was going to take Sierra on a walk before Dog Club?" I asked, my eyes on my uneaten plate of chicken.

"Yes, to help her calm down a bit at the shelter," my mom said.

"Yeah, well, I lost her," I said, the words painful to say out loud. "Her leash slipped out of my hands and she ran away."

"Oh no," my mom said.

"We found her and she's fine," I said. "But everyone was pretty worried, especially her owner. It was awful."

"It sounds upsetting," my mom said.

"Alice was so worried—everyone was—and the whole thing was my—" suddenly I choked up and couldn't go on. I'd held in my tears all afternoon but I couldn't keep them back one second longer.

"Honey, wait," my mom called as I pushed back my chair and ran from the table. But I didn't stop. I ran up the stairs and threw myself down on my bed, crying and crying. I kept feeling Sierra's leash slip through my fingers, seeing the empty street where she'd disappeared, and worst off all, the faces of Alice, Mr. Finnegan, Tim, Caley, and my friends—all of them so anxious, all because of me. My mom had been right: I was way too flighty and forgetful to ever be able to take care of anything.

I stood up, my face wet with tears, and grabbed the file filled with pet quizzes and magazines from my desk, then stuffed them in the trash. I wasn't responsible enough for a pet, so there was no point in keeping them.

Today had shown me that once and for all.

Two days later, when it was time to return to the shelter, I told Kim and Taylor that my stomach was hurting so I couldn't go. It was pretty much the truth; ever since I'd lost Sierra there had been a hard pit in the center of my belly that made me ache.

"Sash, the dogs will miss you," Taylor said as we walked out of school together. There was a brisk wind and the crisp smell of falling leaves in the air—a perfect day to play with dogs.

"Especially Mr. Smashmouth," Kim added.

My heart twisted at the thought of missing time with my beloved little buddy but I couldn't bear seeing Alice, Tim, or Caley, not after what had happened. "I'll see him next week," I said as we reached the corner.

They both hugged me, then headed reluctantly to pick up their club dogs and mine while I walked home, alone.

It felt strange to be in our house so early. I almost wasn't sure what I should do. Finally I headed into the kitchen to fix a snack. Just as I was slicing some cheese, I heard the front door open.

"Mom?" I asked. I mean, of course it had to be her—we didn't hand out copies of our key to ax murderers or anything. But it was strange for her to be home so early too.

"Hi, Sash," she said, walking into the kitchen. Her burgundy suit looked as neat as it had when she'd left this morning. "What are you doing home?"

"I didn't feel like going to the shelter today," I admitted. She'd tried to get me to talk after I'd had my meltdown the other night but I hadn't been up to getting into it then, or yesterday when she asked me about it again. But now I was ready to have her ask more about what had happened and how I was doing.

"Are you sick?" she asked, checking the clock on the stove instead of looking at me. She was clearly distracted and my urge to talk withered away.

"Just a little stomachache," I said. Then I realized I had a big snack sitting in front of me.

But my mom didn't seem to notice. "Okay, well, I have some calls to make," she said. "And I was thinking to just put together a big salad for dinner, does that sound okay?"

"Sure," I said listlessly. "I can help."

"That would be great," she said, planting a kiss on my head and then going to her home office.

I put my snack away. Somehow the talk with my mom had killed my appetite. Instead I headed upstairs to finish my homework, alone.

"I think we're done," Kim said, surveying the three baking pans sitting on the counter in Taylor's kitchen.

Our latest batch of Turkish delight was cooling inside them.

"It sure smells good in here," Taylor's dad said, coming in with a bag from Old Farm Market.

"Hi, Mr. Burke," Kim and I both said as he set the groceries down on the island in the middle of their sunny kitchen, which was perfumed with lemon and rose from our candy.

"We're glad to have you ladies with us tonight," he said. His Southern accent was even stronger and more musical than Taylor's. "I'll be whipping up a batch of my famous fried chicken and grits."

"Dad, I think they're only famous under our roof," Taylor said playfully.

"No, they're legendary," Mr. Burke said confidently. "Known throughout the land."

Taylor rolled her eyes but Kim laughed and I managed a smile. I still felt the heaviness of losing Sierra hanging over me and even the fun of cooking with my friends couldn't erase it.

"Let me know when I can take over in here," he said.

"It's all yours," Taylor said. She kissed him on the cheek as we headed out.

Taylor lived in an old Victorian house with uneven wooden floors and rooms painted surprising colors, like the bright orange hall that led to the stairs. Taylor's sisters Tasha and Jasmine, twins, were coming down the stairs, both dressed for their weekend jobs. Tasha worked at the Roxbury Park Cineplex while Jasmine had a job almost as cool as ours, selling candy at Sugar and Spice on Main Street. They were juniors in high school and Taylor got along with them pretty well. It was just Anna who really grated on her.

"You can use my manicure kit if you make sure to put everything back," Tasha told Taylor, smiling at me and Kim.

"And I'll bring you guys back some chocolate popcorn balls after work," Jasmine promised. The chocolate popcorn balls at Sugar and Spice, which were also dipped in caramel, were amazing.

"Thanks," we all said as they headed out.

"Your sisters are so nice," Kim said.

But then Anna appeared at the top of the stairs, hands on her hips. "You left your wet towel on the bathroom floor," she accused Taylor. "*Again.*"

"That was hours ago," Taylor huffed. "Get over it."

Anna looked ready to go off but we hustled up the stairs and slipped into Taylor's room fast.

"She drives me crazy," Taylor said with a sigh as she flopped onto her bed, which was covered with a bright turquoise quilt.

"She seemed mad," Kim said, biting her lip.

"She's always mad about something," Taylor said. "But don't worry. I already asked and she's happy to help you study for math."

"That's great," Kim said, relieved.

"She'd never pass up an opportunity to show off her math genius," Taylor groused. "Though I guess in this case it's a good thing."

Kim settled on the end of Taylor's bed while I sat

down in the papasan chair she had nestled in one corner. Taylor's room was painted a cheerful raspberry and most of the wall space was covered with photos she'd taken. My favorite was her section from the Dog Club, with candid shots of us playing with the dogs. Though today I avoided looking at it. I wasn't ready to think about the shelter.

But then Kim cleared her throat and looked at me. "Sash, you need to stop feeling bad about what happened with Sierra," she said. "Honestly it could have been any of us and the same thing would have happened."

"She's right," Taylor said, propping herself up on one elbow and looking at me earnestly. "Sierra's so wild something like that was bound to happen at some point."

Their words comforted me but I still wasn't completely convinced. "It was my idea for us to walk her though," I said. "And that was what made it so bad."

"At least you tried to come up with a plan to help,"

Taylor pointed out. "I just hid from her!"

I laughed for the first time since Sierra had gone missing.

"You know, the problem isn't you or any of us," Taylor went on. "It's Sierra. I've been thinking about it and I'm starting to agree with Alice: Sierra just isn't a good fit for our Dog Club."

I was shocked. "But our club is supposed to be for all dogs."

Kim leaned forward and I turned toward her, ready to hear her agree with me. "Actually I think Taylor's right," she said.

My mouth fell open. Kim, dog whisperer extraordinaire, thought there was a dog we couldn't handle?

"At first I thought it would be giving up to tell the Finnegans Sierra couldn't come to the club anymore," Kim continued, twisting a lock of her hair as she spoke. "And I worried it would be bad for our business."

"I'm worried about that too," I jumped in.

"But I realized it's not true," Kim said. "We're not

helping Sierra or our business by letting things continue like this. She's stressing everyone out and we're neglecting the other dogs. And that will hurt the Dog Club more than anything else."

I'd never thought of it like that.

"I think the Finnegans will understand," Taylor said. "I mean, they see how wild she is at the shelter. Honestly at this point they're probably expecting it."

"They can find something that's a better fit for Sierra," Kim said. "And we can keep the club a safe place for the dogs we can manage. I think asking Sierra to leave is the most responsible thing we can do."

At that I burst into tears.

For a moment Kim and Taylor were frozen. Then they both jumped up and rushed over to me, putting their arms around me in a very squishy hug.

"I'm sorry," I managed to choke out.

"Don't be sorry," Kim said.

"Just tell us what's wrong," Taylor added. "So we can fix it."

I really had the best friends ever.

I pulled myself together, accepting a tissue from the box Taylor held out to me, and wiping my face. Then I looked at my friends. "It's about being responsible," I said. "And how I'm not."

"Wait, what?" Taylor asked, looking thoroughly confused.

"You know how my mom won't let me get a pet?" I asked, sniffing a little.

"Right, because they're too messy," Kim said, nodding.

"That's the thing though," I said. "It's not just that pets are messy. It's that my mom doesn't think I'm responsible enough to take care of a pet."

There was silence and for a moment I thought my friends agreed with her.

But then Kim spoke. "She's wrong," she said forcefully.

"Totally wrong," Taylor added. "You're one of the most responsible people I know."

"I'm not though," I said. "Like just think how often I forget my backpack or my shelter clothes."

"That's being forgetful about stuff that doesn't matter that much," Taylor said. "Not being irresponsible."

"I lost Sierra," I pointed out. "Totally irresponsible."

"No," Kim said, shaking her head. "Like Taylor said before, you were trying to solve a big problem in our business. That's being responsible."

"You take good care of the dogs at the shelter," Taylor said.

"Yeah, but I love doing that," I said. "It doesn't count as work."

"You never miss a dance rehearsal," Kim added.

"I love dance too," I pointed out. "And anyway, my mom drives me to class."

"You made sure we got every step of the Turkish delight recipe right today," Taylor said.

"That's because you told me to be in charge of reading the recipe," I said.

"And you never forget the stuff that really matters,

like sleepover milk shakes," Kim said.

"She's right," Taylor said. "If you hadn't reminded me we might not have enough ice cream or M&M's for tonight. And that would be a tragedy!"

We laughed at that.

"Thanks, you guys," I said. What they said made me feel at least a little better, but it still didn't convince me that I really was responsible. Sierra had gotten lost on my watch and nothing anyone said could change that.

14

It was last period and I watched the minutes tick down, wishing the final bell would never ring. Today would be my first day back at the shelter and I didn't feel ready to face Alice, Tim, and Caley. But going to the shelter was my job and I knew it was time to go back, even if the thought of it made my stomach feel like the inside of a washing machine.

There was a knock on the door of my math class and a second later a student aide popped in. "Sasha Brown needs to come down to the office," she said.

Kim and Taylor looked over in alarm as I gathered up my stuff with shaking hands. Had something happened to my mom?

I rushed down the hall as fast as I could without technically running. Okay, maybe I ran a little, but I was scared. I never got called down to the office.

"Is everything okay?" I asked as soon as I burst into the big room, which always smelled like musty paper and coffee.

Mr. Mayfield, the administrative assistant sitting behind the counter, nodded. "Everything's fine, Sasha," he said. "I just had a call from your mom and she wants you to go straight home after school. But she said to be sure to tell you it wasn't an emergency, so don't worry."

"Oh, okay," I said, puzzled. "Thanks."

The final bell rang and I headed over to my locker, where Kim and Taylor were already waiting for me.

"Is everything okay?" Kim asked anxiously.

"I think so," I said. "It was just a message from my mom saying I need to go straight home but that it wasn't an emergency."

"Phew," Taylor said. "I was worried."

"Me too," I said.

Kim checked her watch. "We should get going since we'll need to get Gus too," she said to Taylor. "Sash, text us as soon as you know what's going on."

"Okay," I said, pulling books out of my locker and stuffing them in my backpack. I knew my mom had said it wasn't an emergency but I couldn't help being nervous. What was going on that I had to go straight home?

And then, with sickening certainty, I realized: Alice must have called my mom to tell her that I couldn't work at the shelter anymore. It only made sense that after I'd actually lost one of the dogs she couldn't afford to have me work there. As the truth of this sank in, I leaned against my locker, my legs suddenly too shaky to hold me up. What would I do without the Dog Club?

For a terrible moment I thought I might start crying right there in the hall. But then Rachel and Emily yelled good-bye to me as they passed and I managed to straighten up and make my way out the door, toward home. There was no point in putting it off. I'd just hear my mom say it, then lock myself in my room for the rest of my life.

But when I actually got to my house I couldn't make myself walk up the front steps. I loved the shelter and my dog time more than anything. I couldn't bear to have it taken away. There had to be *something* I could do to convince Alice to give me another shot. But then I remembered how distressed she'd been when Sierra was missing. How could I ever make up for that?

I knew my mom was waiting so finally I dragged myself up to the front door, my feet like lead and my stomach hollow.

This was going to be the worst moment of my life.

"Hi, honey," my mom called, sounding breathless and even a bit happy as I turned my key and opened the door. I must have been hearing wrong though—no doubt she was totally upset I'd been fired from the shelter and the Dog Club I'd helped to start. "You forgot something."

That gave me pause. My shelter clothes were in my bag, so what could I have forgotten? And what did that have to do with Alice telling me not to come to the shelter anymore?

"What?" I asked, following the sound of her voice to the kitchen.

When I got there I stopped in my tracks, unable to register what I was seeing. In fact, I had to be imagining things. Because there was no way Mr. Smashmouth could be here, in my house.

"Surprise!" my mom called out, her eyes shining.

But I couldn't really and truly believe it until Mr. Smashmouth himself had run over to me and began bouncing joyfully at my feet, yipping in delight. I scooped him up and cuddled him close. "Mom, what's going on?" I asked, my voice high and breathy, the way game-show winners sounded when they'd landed the big prize.

"Well, I just needed you to come by to get Mr. Smashmouth for Dog Club," she said. "He wouldn't want to miss it. But don't forget to bring him with you when you come home—he lives with us now."

It was so incredibly wonderful I couldn't even speak.

"It's true, Sash," she said, coming over and wrapping an arm around me and Mr. Smashmouth. "I called Alice yesterday and went in this morning to finish the paperwork. We've officially adopted Mr. Smashmouth."

So that was why my mom had been on the phone yesterday. I thought she'd been distracted by work and ignoring me when in fact she was making my dream come true.

"Mom, thank you!" I exclaimed, throwing an arm around her, Mr. Smashmouth pressed between us. He responded by giving each of us kisses.

"You guys better get going," my mom said affectionately. "You don't want to be late for Dog Club."

I walked out into the front hall, where I saw a few additions I'd missed on the way in, like a hook for Mr. Smashmouth's leash, a dog mat, and a newly installed Dustbuster just inside the door. If my mom was already prepping the cleaning for dog fur and dirt tracked in by little white paws, Mr. Smashmouth really and truly did live with us!

I'd thought I was walking in to the worst moment of my life—how wrong I'd been!

I turned and threw my arms around my mom again. "This is the best day ever," I told her, nearly tearful with joy. "Thank you!"

When I got to the shelter with Mr. Smashmouth a few minutes later everyone began to cheer. Alice's face was shining, Caley was beaming, Tim was pumping a fist in the air, and Taylor and Kim raced over to hug me and my dog—how I loved the sound of those words! Even the other dogs sensed the excitement and were bouncing around happily.

Alice came over and rested a hand on Mr. Smashmouth, who was snug in my arms. "I'm usually both happy and sad when a dog gets adopted from the shelter," she said. "Because I want the dogs to find homes but I miss having them here. But this is perfect—Mr. Smashmouth has a home and we still get to see him at Dog Club!"

"Yes, we'd miss you too much if you were gone for good," Caley said to Mr. Smashmouth. Then she gave me a squeeze. "I'm so thrilled for you, Sash," she said. "I know how much you love this little guy."

"I still kind of can't believe it," I said.

"You finally got your dog," Kim said, with a grin.

"And not to say I told you so," Taylor began, "but clearly Kim and I were totally right."

"About what?" I asked, confused.

"About you being responsible, of course," Taylor said. "It might have taken your mom a bit, but we saw it all along."

Boxer bounded over with his Frisbee and Coco

raced to Kim's feet with a tennis ball. As we settled into a happy afternoon of playing I contemplated what Taylor had said. My mom must have decided I was responsible or she wouldn't have gotten me the best pet in the world. But what had changed her mind? Sure, I'd gone on a campaign to show her I had changed, but nearly everything I'd done had backfired. So why had my mom decided I was ready for a pet now?

15

"Welcome to the Ottoman Empire," Mr. Martin declared grandly, from the stage in the auditorium. "Your time machine has taken you back to an age of politics, art, and unbridled discovery. Walk around, embrace this amazing culture, and enjoy your visit to the past!"

"That was a little much," Dana said. She, Rachel, Emily, and Naomi stood next to us, wearing leotards and draped in scarves they'd borrowed from their moms for their Ottoman dance.

"Oh, it's sweet how excited he gets," Emily said with a smile.

Naomi rolled her eyes but I kind of agreed with Emily—the whole room was bustling with kids in costume, large art displays, performance areas and, of course, food.

"I hear Alec and Danny are performing an epic poem," Taylor said. "That I want to see."

"Forget poetry," Naomi said, rubbing her hands together. "I want to try your candy!"

We led them over to our display on Turkish delight, passing Sofia and Jade, who were singing Ottoman folk songs, and the puppet show that Carmen, Terrell, and Marlena were performing. Their projects were good but so was ours—I was really proud of how it had turned out. The posters explaining the history of the delight, facts about Ottoman cuisine, and dining customs looked sleek and were packed with cool facts. The candy was perfect, cut into bite-size squares and set on silver trays my mom had gotten out of the attic to make it look extra fancy. Not that our classmates cared so much about that. They were just excited to get candy in school!

"This is delish," Rachel said after taking a delicate bite.

"Hey, candy!" Dennis called to Alec and Danny. The three of them nearly shoved Rachel over as they rushed for the trays.

"It's like a pack of wild dogs," Taylor muttered to me and Kim as the boys dug into the candy.

"Just one per person," Kim called, to no avail.

"Gentlemen, I fear you've forgotten your manners," Mr. Martin said as he came up from behind us. "Though I certainly understand your enthusiasm. Turkish delight is a true delicacy. I'm thrilled to learn more about it."

The boy pack headed to the next food booth while Mr. Martin began reading our posters. Taylor was helping Rachel set up the music for their dance in the space next to us but Kim was rooted to the spot, her whole body tense as Mr. Martin looked over our work. I put a hand on her shoulder and we waited together, the sounds of laughter, exotic music, and a few scraps of poetry floating around us.

Finally Mr. Martin picked up a slice of our Turkish delight and popped it into his mouth. "Delicious," he proclaimed. "And your posters are top-notch. Your group has earned an A."

Kim was beaming and as soon as he'd moved on she let out a squeal. "My parents are going to be so proud!"

"My mom too," I said, thinking of how fun it would be to tell her and Mr. Smashmouth about the festival. Knowing I was going home to my beloved dog made the whole day special.

"And once again I was right," Taylor said. She'd come back in time to hear our grade. "I said we'd knock his socks off and that's exactly what we did."

"I guess we just need to accept that you're all-knowing," Kim said with an easy grin. It was nice to see her so relaxed.

"You finally get it," Taylor said.

And we all laughed at that.

"Mom, you got butterscotch sauce for the milk shakes, right?" I asked. We were in the kitchen together, preparing a big feast of spaghetti and meatballs that was going to be followed by my mother's famous chocolate cake, the one she only baked for the most special occasions. Like tonight, when we were celebrating our newest family member, who was sitting on his dog bed in the corner while my mom and I bustled about.

"Hon, do you really think you girls will want milk shakes after all this food?" my mom asked.

My face fell but before I could say anything she laughed. "I'm just teasing," she said. "I know you girls need your milk shakes for sleepovers. I got everything, don't worry."

My mom was seriously the best.

"You know, you never told me what happened with Sierra," my mom said as she took the lid off a pot of boiling water and put in the spaghetti.

"We talked with Alice and the Finnegans and all of us decided Sierra would be better off not being in the Dog Club," I said. My job was stirring the bubbling tomato sauce, which smelled divine.

"That sounds like the right choice," my mom said.

It *had* been the right choice. The Finnegans totally agreed and weren't upset at all. And Dog Club had been much better without Sierra disrupting things. I'd been so worried about not doing a good job when in fact, in this case, the best job was to admit we couldn't handle Sierra. It had seemed like giving up when really it was actually the responsible thing to do. Which reminded me of the question I'd been meaning to ask my mom.

"Why did you decide we should adopt Mr. Smashmouth?" I asked. "I mean, why now?"

My mom was near Mr. Smashmouth's bed and she paused to rub his ears. It was awesome to see how much she loved him!

"Well, it was obvious to me that you were ready,"

she said, giving Mr. Smashmouth one more pat before standing up. "I saw that you were responsible enough to handle taking care of a pet, and I knew this little guy was the one you wanted."

I remembered the day she had come into the shelter and seen me with Mr. Smashmouth. But I still had questions. "I don't want to disagree or anything," I said. "But it actually seems like everything I've done lately just proves how scatterbrained I am. Like the mess with the Turkish delight and losing Sierra."

My mom shook her head. "No, it's the opposite," she said. "Those were some of the things that showed me how responsible you'd become."

"Really?" I asked incredulously.

"Yes," she said firmly. "Being responsible isn't just making the right choice and having everything go perfectly. It's also how you handle the things that go wrong."

"I never thought of it like that," I said.

"Like with the Turkish delight," she said. "You guys

had an accident that caused a huge mess, but you didn't try to cover it up. You owned up to what happened and you worked your tail off to help me clean it."

I had worked hard—my arms had even been sore the next day.

"And with Sierra, not only did you work to find a solution to a pretty big problem," she said, "but as soon as she went missing you did everything possible to make sure she was found. And once she was, you apologized and took responsibility for your mistake. You didn't try to hide your part in what went wrong and you were willing to take any consequences that came your way."

"I guess that's true," I said slowly. It was strange to say, but I was starting to see what she meant. And realize, for the very first time, that maybe I wasn't so scatterbrained after all.

"Thanks, Mom," I said.

Just then the doorbell rang and Mr. Smashmouth jumped up with a happy bark, ready to greet our guests.

"Sounds like your friends are here," my mom said.

"And dinner's just about ready. Let's start celebrating!"

As I headed down the hall, Mr. Smashmouth prancing cheerfully at my heels, I couldn't help thinking how much I had to celebrate: my friends, my new dog, and my mom truly believing in me.

Really, what more could a girl ever want?

KEEP READING FOR A SNEAK PEEK AT THE NEXT DOG CLUB ADVENTURE!

Taylor is amazed at how quickly Roxbury Park has started to feel like home, but not everyone is as welcoming as Kim and Sasha. Lately she's been getting picked on for being the new girl at school. And Taylor isn't the only one under attack—the Dog Club is facing some serious competition. Is there only room for one top dog in Roxbury Park?

1

"See you tomorrow, Taylor," my friend Rachel said as we passed in the hall after the final bell. People streamed by as I waved to her and then turned in to my locker alcove and began to twirl my lock.

In some ways I was still getting used to Roxbury Park Middle School. Well, everyone in my class was, really, since it was our first year of middle school. But it was also my first year living in Roxbury Park and it still amazed me how fast it had become home. I'd lived my whole life in Greensboro, North Carolina, and when my dad announced we were moving to Illinois so he could work with an old law school friend at her firm, I cried for days. I was sure my life was over. But fast-forward two months and I had a whole new life that I loved just as much as my old one, maybe even more. Roxbury Park was a pretty, friendly town; I had two fabulous best friends; and I was a proud founding member of the Roxbury Park Dog Club. What more could a girl ask for?

"Nice shirt," someone sneered behind me. I didn't have to turn around to know it was Brianna Chen mocking what I thought was just a basic pink T-shirt.

Okay, so there was one thing I could ask for in my new life: for Brianna Chen to stop bothering me. It had started a few weeks ago: a snippy remark here, a put-down there. I kept thinking she'd get over it and find someone else to bug, but so far no luck. If anything, it was getting worse.

I sucked in my breath and turned to face her.

Brianna was Asian, with long hair, tanned skin, and a perfect fashion sense. Today she was wearing jean capris, a shimmery black shirt, and delicate silver sandals that would have given me blisters after ten minutes.

"I guess girls still wear pink where you're from, New Girl?" Brianna asked airily. She made "New Girl" sound like a gross skin disease.

"Um, yeah," I said. I never knew how to respond to Brianna's insults. I mean, how do you defend the color pink when you don't even know what's wrong with it in the first place?

Brianna raised an eyebrow, her upper lip crinkling as though just being near my pink shirt was enough to give her hives. "You might want to get rid of it now that you live here," Brianna said, smoothing a lock of sleek black hair behind one ear. "Maybe give it to a first grader or something."

I didn't know what to say but it didn't matter because Brianna had turned on her heel and was marching away, a small smile on her face.

I looked down at my shirt, which was the cheerful color of bubble gum, and tried to promise myself that I'd still wear it, that I wouldn't let Brianna's words ruin it for me. But deep down I knew they already had and that my shirt would be staying home from now on. Which was a drag because I really liked it—my sister Jasmine gave it to me because she said this color looked good with my brown skin and black hair. But I had a lot of other shirts, and it would probably be getting too cold for T-shirts soon anyway.

"Ready to go?"

This time the voice behind me made me smile. "Sure am," I said, shutting my locker and hoisting my backpack over my shoulder. Sasha, my best friend, her brown curls popping out of her ponytail, was grinning at me as she played with a strap on her backpack.

"Let's go get Kim," she said. "She wanted to talk to Mr. Martin about the test tomorrow, so I said we'd meet her at her locker."